UNSOLVED TRUE CRIME TALES

Featuring cases from across the 19th & 20th century

Adrian Finney

Strange Britain

Copyright © 2026 Adrian Finney - Strange Britain

Copyright © 2025 Adrian Finney - Strange Britain
All rights reserved

No part of this book may be reproduced, or stored in a retrieval system,
or transmitted in any form or by any means, electronic, mechanical,
photocopying, recording, or otherwise, without express written
permission of the publisher.

Cover design by: Adrian Finney

strangebritain.eventbrite.com

facebook.com/strangebritain
strangebritain.org.uk
strangebritainofficial@gmail.com

CONTENTS

Title Page

Copyright

Introduction

The Girl in the Locked Room (Or, Trial by Tabloid) — 1

The Man Behind the Pretty Windows (Or, Death by Kaleidoscope Light) — 6

The Man from the Prudential (A Locked Room Murder, An Impossible Address, & The Naked Mackintosh) — 12

The Field of the Dead (Or, Manchester's Dirty Secret) — 30

The Pusher (Or, History Repeating Down by the Irk) — 35

The View from the Carriage (Or, Murder in Passing) — 40

The Draper's Last Customer (Or, Murder by the Yard) — 46

The Bonfire of Identity (Or, The Man Who Wasn't There)	51
The Final Reel (Or, Death in the Cinema)	55
The Man Above the Laundry (Or, The Steam That Hid the Blood)	59
The Red Shoe (Or, The Cinderella of Tang Hall)	65
The Silence of Moss Side (Or, The Man Who Talked Too Much)	71
The Stationmaster's Last Shift (Or, A Ticket to Nowhere)	77
The Vase on the Mantelpiece (Or, The Quiet Death of a Quiet Man)	84
The Girl in the Tree (Or, How to Hide a Body in the West Midlands)	89
The Girl in the Burning Car (Or, The Man in the Bowler Hat)	97
The Saint in the Dance Hall (Or, Saturday Night Fever with a Vengeance)	104
The Left Luggage (Or, The Girl with the Dancer's Legs)	113
The Man Who Didn't Do It (Or, The Scottish Dreyfuss)	119
The Man Without a Name (Or, The Harvest of Bone)	126
The Girl on the Shore (Or, The Silence of Leith)	133

The Girl in the Cave (Or, The Long Wait at Brandy Cove)	139
The Judge's Daughter (Or, Murder at The Glen)	145
The Black Dahlia	153
Afterword	175

INTRODUCTION

I was probably seven or eight when I realised monsters were real.

They weren't hiding under the bed or in the wardrobe. They were sitting on a shelf in a cheap book shop in Nottingham city centre, sandwiched between cookbooks and travel guides. They were trapped inside cheaply printed, pocket money priced, books with titles that screamed in bold: The World's Greatest Serial Killers. The World's Greatest Unsolved Crimes.

I was far too young to be reading them. That, of course, was exactly why I had to have them. If a bookshop today sold a book like that to a child? It would be front page news – with screams of "Protect our Children!"

But in the early 1990s? I was sold those books, no questions asked. The shop is now long gone, as is the Broadmarsh shopping centre where it was located, but the memory remains

I remember the smell of those books—that specific scent of cheap laminate and old paper. I remember the weight of them in my hands. But mostly, I remember the feeling of opening them and stepping into a world that felt illicit, terrifying, and completely magnetic.

For a child, true crime is a strange thing. At that age, you don't fully grasp the permanency of death or the sheer devastation of grief. Instead, these books presented murder as a kind of dark mythology. The killers were presented almost like comic book villains. They had nicknames: Jack The Ripper. The Night Stalker. They had kill counts and "hunting grounds."

I came of age in Nottingham at the turn of the 21st century. It was a complicated time for the city. To the rest of the country, we had a reputation; the tabloids had branded us with the grim moniker of "Shottingham," painting a picture of a city under siege by gun crime and gang violence. For a teenager living there, it felt different—it was just home—but there was an undercurrent of tension, a sense that the violence you read about in books wasn't always confined to history or far-off American highways.

Hearing gunshots on a night out was not uncommon but, perhaps with the naivety of youth shining through, I assumed I'd be safe. The bars and pubs that were magnets for violence didn't play my kind of music so I'd be fine...

Then, the reality of it landed on my doorstep.

In September 2003, a jeweller named Marian Bates was murdered during a robbery gone wrong. It didn't happen in a dark alley in Victorian London or a vacant lot in LA. It happened in a shop less than half a mile from where I grew up.

At the time, I was in Birmingham's Royal Orthopaedic Hospital, recovering from a limb salvage operation, after the removal of a rare form of bone cancer in my leg.

As I lay on the ward, watching what should have been yet another daytime TV show about estate agents in badly fitting suits, they cut to a live bulletin. It was breaking news coverage, and there was something familiar, a small shop framed behind police tape.

I knew that shop. I had been inside countless times. I had stood at the counter and bought presents for my family. It was a shop full of memories. When the victim was identified as Marian it stuck me. She wasn't a character in a book; she was a real person with a kind face and a job to do. When the news broke, the shock was physical. It stripped away the safety glass that I had built up through years of reading crime encyclopedias.

Suddenly, murder wasn't a "case study." It wasn't a puzzle to be solved by a detective with a drinking problem. It was the shuttered shop down the road. It was the flowers piling up on the pavement.

Over time, that experience would come to change how I looked at the books on my shelf.

I went back to those old volumes, in fact I still have them to this day. I went to the chapter on Los Angeles in the 1940s. I turned the page and found myself staring at the famous black-and-white photograph of the Black Dahlia.

I remember the shock of it hitting me differently this time. I looked at the grain, high-contrast photo of Elizabeth Short's body in the weeds, and I didn't see a "mystery." I saw someone who had been young, who had been scared, just as Marian Bates had been.

I realised then that the books had lied to me. They were breathless, almost excited. They revelled in the gore. They treated the mutilation as a "masterpiece" of crime and the victim as a prop in a noir detective story.

In the books, we're urged to play armchair detective, pouring over suspect lists and dubious evidence. In real life, no one was ever charged with Marion's death, though the local belief was that her killers were themselves dead within a few hours at the hands of a local gang boss.

That sensationalism never again sat right with me. It also planted the first seeds of an idea that would take almost two decades to come to fruition.

It has been a long two decades. I was lucky in that my cancer surgery was a success but the path to recovery was long and I think I lost myself a fair few times along the way.

During the first Covid lockdown I rediscovered a passion for writing, and it led to my first book, on local folklore. That ultimately led to my dream job, running Sheffield's Ghost Tours, as a professional storyteller.

It's a job in which I feel I've finally recovered a version of me that died, back in 2003, whilst undergoing cancer treatment. I'd lost my confidence, my spark, something innate that made me who I was.

But in my slow recovery, and then in rediscovering a passion for writing, and also finding a hitherto unknown passion for performing, I found myself.

In the tail end of 2022, I decided that I wanted to revisit true crime, for a Valentine's special live event. But I wanted to handle the stories my way, to place the victims at the heart of the coverage, and to focus on the very human forces that drive some to commit horrible acts.

It was a proof of concept idea, one that saw me contact dozens of venues, trying to convince them that true crime would be a popular idea for a night.

The night sold out, and people responded warmly to that more human take on true crime, and it's against that backdrop that this project was born.

The stories collected here are not about glorifying the act of murder. They are about the atmosphere of the time. They are about the cities that allowed these things to happen—the fog of Victorian London, the steam of the railways, the desperate poverty of Angel Meadow, and the neon shadows of 1940s Los Angeles.

I wanted to revisit these cases—some famous, many forgotten—and strip away the sensationalism. I wanted to write about them not as "plots," but as tragedies.

Writing these stories has been a journey back to that bookshelf in my childhood bedroom. But this time, I am reading between the lines. I am looking for the people who were erased.

We all have a shared interest in the shocking acts that humans commit. It is part of our survival instinct to study the predator. But we also have a responsibility to the prey.

So, let us head into the dark together. But let us do it with our eyes open, and with a promise: we are not here to celebrate monsters. We are here to remember the lives they tried to extinguish.

Welcome to the shadows. Watch your step.

THE GIRL IN THE LOCKED ROOM (OR, TRIAL BY TABLOID)

London, 1907

On a warm September morning in 1907, Camden Town was waking up. In those days, Camden wasn't the land of Doc Martens, overpriced street food, and tourists looking for Amy Winehouse's favourite pub. It was a place of steam trains, horse manure, and the kind of crushing, soot-stained poverty that looks charming in a Dickens adaptation but smells terrible in real life.

At 29 Agar Grove, however, the morning routine had been violently interrupted. Behind the ground floor door lay Emily Dimmock. She was twenty-two. She was known to her friends as "Pretty Polly." And she had been dead for hours.

Her throat had been cut so efficiently that the bedclothes were soaked through, yet the room was eerily undisturbed. There was no broken glass, no overturned chair, no sign of the desperate struggle you might expect. It was a quiet, domestic apocalypse.

Almost immediately, the case stopped being a police investigation and started being a national spectator sport. This was the Camden Town Murder, the case that would teach the British press exactly how profitable a dead girl could be.

Emily Dimmock lived in the grey area of Edwardian

morality. She was a part-time prostitute, a fact that the newspapers would later clutch their pearls over while simultaneously printing every salacious detail they could find.

She shared her lodgings with Robert Wood. Wood was a commercial artist, a man of some education, and —if we are being charitable—a bit of a narcissist. Their relationship was "bohemian," which is the polite historical code for "they weren't married, they shouted a lot, and the neighbours pressed glasses to the wall to listen."

On the morning of September 12, Emily's neighbour, Elizabeth Jones, noticed the silence. When the door was finally breached, the police found Emily. The killer had locked the door from the outside and vanished into the London smog.

The police arrived and did what police in 1907 usually did: they searched for the boyfriend.

Robert Wood was not in the room. He hadn't been there all night. This, combined with the fact that he had once reportedly told an acquaintance, "If I can't have her, no one shall," made him the only suspect that mattered. It didn't help that Wood had asked friends to provide him with a false alibi for the night in question—a move that usually screams "guilty" to a jury.

He was arrested. The police rubbed their hands together. Case closed, surely? If this murder had happened ten years earlier, Robert Wood would likely have hanged quietly. But 1907 was the dawn of the mass media age. The newspapers realized that the Camden Town Murder had the "Holy Trinity" of readership engagement: Sex, Violence, and Class.

They went berserk. They printed diagrams of the

bedroom. They analysed the blood spatter. They turned Robert Wood into a celebrity monster. He was painted as a jealous brute, a man whose artistic temperament concealed a murderous rage. But there was a problem. The more the press screamed, the more the actual evidence began to look like Swiss cheese.

Problem One: The Weapon

To cut a throat as deeply as Emily's was cut, you need a serious knife. It would be covered in blood. The killer would be covered in blood. Yet, no knife was found. No bloody clothes were found in Wood's possession. He couldn't very well have eaten the knife, and he certainly didn't have time to scrub a crime scene to forensic perfection.

Problem Two: The Timeline

Medical science in 1907 was more "educated guessing" than CSI. They knew Emily died at night, but they couldn't prove when. Wood had a shaky alibi, but he wasn't invisible.

Problem Three: The Other Men

Emily was a sex worker. She had clients. Lots of them. Witnesses reported seeing her with a "mystery man" shortly before she died. Another spoke of a man leaving the house in a hurry. The police, suffering from a classic case of tunnel vision, largely ignored these leads. Why hunt for a phantom stranger when you have a boyfriend who writes incriminating letters?

The trial at the Old Bailey was less of a legal proceeding and more of a theatrical production. The public gallery was packed with ladies in hats and gentlemen with opera glasses, all hoping to catch a glimpse of the killer.

The prosecution played their hand: Wood was jealous,

Wood was unstable, Wood was there. But the defence, led by the legendary Edward Marshall Hall, played a better one. Marshall Hall was the kind of barrister who could make a jury weep over a parking ticket. He didn't try to prove Wood was a saint; he just had to prove he wasn't a murderer.

He leaned into the lack of physical evidence. He pointed out the sheer impossibility of Wood walking through Camden covered in blood without anyone noticing. He argued that Emily, by nature of her profession, let dangerous men into her room as a matter of course.

And then, Robert Wood took the stand. Usually, accused murderers are told to sit down and shut up. Wood, however, was enjoying the attention. He was articulate, somewhat arrogant, yet strangely charming. He admitted to being a fool. He admitted to asking for a false alibi because he was terrified of being involved. But he looked the jury in the eye and swore he didn't kill her.

The jury deliberated. The tension in the room was thick enough to cut with the knife they never found.

Verdict: Not Guilty.

The courtroom erupted. People cheered. Wood was carried out on the shoulders of the crowd like a football hero. It was a stunning rebuke of the police and a reminder that being a bad boyfriend doesn't necessarily make you a killer.

Robert Wood, free but forever tainted, changed his name and vanished into obscurity, dying decades later in a quiet corner of England.

But the case refused to die. It became a cultural ghost. It famously obsessed the painter Walter Sickert. Sickert painted a series of works titled The Camden Town

Murder, depicting a clothed man sitting on a bed next to a naked, reclining woman. The paintings are moody, ambiguous, and deeply unsettling.

Decades later, the crime novelist Patricia Cornwell would try to argue that Sickert himself was Jack the Ripper and that the Camden murder was part of his portfolio. While this makes for a great book sales pitch, most historians regard it as absolute nonsense.

So, who killed Pretty Polly?

It was almost certainly a client. A nameless man who walked out of the London fog, paid for a service, committed an atrocity, and walked back into the night, shielded by the anonymity that the city provides.

The Camden Town Murder remains unsolved not because it was the perfect crime, but because the police decided they had their man too early, and the press decided the story was better than the truth. In the end, Emily Dimmock became a footnote in her own murder —a prop in a play about male jealousy and media power.

And in 29 Agar Grove, the only witness was the silence.

THE MAN BEHIND THE PRETTY WINDOWS (OR, DEATH BY KALEIDOSCOPE LIGHT)

Nottingham, 1963

If you found yourself in Sneinton, Nottingham, in the early 1960s, you were likely there for one of two reasons: to buy something at the market that fell off the back of a lorry, or to get a drink.

It was a hard-scrabble, working-class district, a place of red brick, industrial soot, and the kind of community spirit that comes from everyone being equally broke. But amidst the grime of Southwell Road, there was a beacon of unexpected beauty.

Officially, the pub was called The Fox and Grapes. But nobody called it that. To the market traders, the factory workers, and the locals wiping the day's dust from their throats, it was simply "Pretty Windows."

The name came from the frontage—an elaborate, multi-coloured expanse of stained glass that looked less like a Nottingham boozer and more like a cathedral dedicated to the worship of mild ale. When the lights were on inside, the pub glowed like a jewel box, casting a kaleidoscopic light onto the pavement. It was a local landmark, a point of pride, and—on a September night in 1963—the backdrop for a murder so savage it would stain the city's history permanently.

The man running the show was George Wilson. By all accounts, George was the archetype of the perfect publican.

He was 60 years old, steady, reliable, and possessed the diplomatic skills required to tell a drunk man it was time to go home without getting a glass in the face.

He lived above the pub with his wife, Betty, and their dog, Blackie. Blackie was a mongrel of indeterminate lineage, the kind of dog that is fiercely loyal and deeply suspicious of postmen.

On the night of September 8, 1963, the rhythm of the evening was the same as it had been for years. The last patron stumbled out, the bolts were thrown across the doors, and the glasses were rinsed. At around 12:30 AM, George prepared for his final ritual of the night: walking Blackie.

It was a simple routine. George would tie the dog's lead to his wrist—a habit born of affection and security—and step out into the cool air of the East Midlands night. He said goodnight to his wife. He stepped out the side door and he never came back.

It only took twenty minutes for the silence of Sneinton to break. Inside the pub, Betty Wilson heard a noise. It wasn't a scream. It was Blackie. The dog was barking with a frantic, rhythmic intensity that signalled something was wrong. Not "there is a cat" wrong, but "the world is ending" wrong.

Betty rushed to the side door and threw it open to find George lying on the pavement. The scene was a chaotic tableau of violence. Beside him lay his keys, scattered like coins. Around him were shards of broken slate, likely dislodged from the low roof during a struggle. And everywhere, there was blood.

George Wilson had been stabbed. Not once, not twice, but fourteen times. This is the detail that stops you cold. A robbery is usually a threat, a scuffle, maybe a single panic-stricken blow. Fourteen stab wounds—to the face, the neck, the back—is not a robbery. It is an execution. It is rage made manifest.

Betty screamed for help, but it was futile. One of the wounds was three and a half inches deep. George Wilson, the man with the steady hand and the pretty windows, was dead before the ambulance could even warm up its engine.

And the killer? He had vanished into the labyrinth of terraced streets, leaving behind a widow, a traumatized dog, and a city that suddenly felt very unsafe.

The Nottingham City Police arrived with the heavy boots and serious faces of men who knew they had a nightmare on their hands. They launched what was, for the time, a massive investigation.

The motive was the first problem. George's wallet was in his pocket. The cash from the till was untouched. So, if it wasn't for money, why kill a beloved 60-year-old landlord?

The police interviewed hundreds of people. They took thousands of statements. But in 1963, forensics was less "CSI: Miami" and more "holding things up to the light and squinting." They didn't have CCTV. They didn't have DNA profiling. They had fingerprints and hunches.

And then, they had the Hitch-hiker. A few days after the murder, a witness came forward with a story that sounded like the beginning of a bad joke. He had picked up a hitch-hiker on the A52, not far from Nottingham.

The man was described as wearing a light-colored raincoat, a scarf, and glasses. On his lapel, he wore a small gold cross. But it was his conversation that raised hairs on the back of the neck. He didn't talk about the football or the weather. He rambled about monasteries. He talked about "God's work." And, bizarrely, he talked about chiropody (foot care).

The police released a sketch. It showed a man who looked like a nervous librarian or a door-to-door evangelist. Was this the face of a man who could stab a landlord fourteen times?

The "religious nutter" theory gained traction. Had George unwittingly offended some wandering zealot? Had the man seen the "Pretty Windows" and mistaken the pub for a church, only to be enraged by the alcohol inside? It was a stretch, but in the absence of facts, the public will happily feast on fiction.

Nine days later, the case got its "smoking gun." Or rather, its rusting blade. Two young boys were playing near Polser Brook—because in the 1960s, children were apparently issued with magnets that attracted them to crime scene evidence. They found a sheath knife dumped in the mud.

The police were ecstatic. The knife was analysed. The blood group on the blade matched George Wilson. The fibres inside the sheath matched George's cardigan.

Case closed? Hardly.

This is where the limitations of the era become painfully clear. Blood grouping is not DNA. George had a common blood type. Millions of men wore cardigans with similar fibres. While it was likely the murder weapon, it couldn't be definitively linked to a specific hand.

Furthermore, if the killer was a random hitch-hiker or a panicked thief, why carry the knife halfway across the city to dump it in a brook? It smacked of local knowledge.

As the weeks turned into months, the investigation stalled, and the rumours began to ferment in the pubs of Nottingham.

Theory One: The Protection Racket

Nottingham has always had a hard edge. In the early 60s, organized crime was muscling in. The theory goes that a local gang demanded George pay for "protection." George, being a stubborn and principled man, told them to get lost. The fourteen stab wounds were a message to every other landlord in the city: Pay up, or get cut.

It fits the violence. It fits the lack of robbery. But George was popular—killing him would bring heat, not compliance.

Theory Two: The "Running Man"

Witnesses reported a man sprinting from the scene, clutching something metallic. He wore a hat and a raincoat, apparently the uniform of the mid-century murderer, and vanished into the shadows of Longden Street. Was he a burglar interrupted? A hitman late for a train? Or just a local running for a bus?

Theory Three: The Caravan of Secrets

Whispers began to circulate about a caravan site in Radcliffe-on-Trent. It was a place known for transients, for people who didn't want to be on the electoral roll. Police raided it. They found burnt-out caravans, which is never a sign of innocent domestic bliss. Was the killer hiding there? Did the "religious hitch-hiker" live off the grid? The trail, like the smoke from the caravans, drifted away into nothing.

Theory Four: The Secret Life

The darkest theory suggests that George wasn't quite the saint everyone thought. Was there a personal grudge? A hidden affair? A debt? Fourteen stab wounds is personal. You don't stab a stranger fourteen times unless you are insane or you hate them with a burning passion. But no evidence of a double life ever surfaced. George appeared to be exactly what he looked like: a decent man, with a loyal dog, who ran a popular pub.

The Pretty Windows murder remains Nottingham's most famous cold case. Betty Wilson never really recovered. How could she? She had opened a door and found her life destroyed on the pavement. She left Sneinton, leaving the ghost of her husband and the beautiful windows behind. She died in 1997, taking her grief, and perhaps her own suspicions, to the grave.

The pub itself survived for decades, though the name changed, and the clientele shifted. But the legend stuck.

In true noir fashion, the tragedy of the Pretty Windows isn't just the death of George Wilson. It's the shattering of the illusion. The stained glass promised warmth and safety. It promised a sanctuary from the grey drudgery of the city. But on that September night, the glass was just a backdrop for a butchery.

Today, modern cold case units occasionally dust off the files.

They look at the sketch of the holy chiropodist. They wonder about the knife in the brook. But the reality is that the killer is likely dead, his secret buried with him in some unmarked grave or crematorium urn.

Nottingham is a city of caves and legends (Robin Hood, anyone?). But the Pretty Windows murder is a different kind of legend. It's a reminder that even in the glow of the most beautiful lights, the darkness is only ever one door, or one shadow, away.

So, if you walk past the old building on Southwell Road, spare a thought for George and Blackie. And remember: if you see a man in a raincoat talking about God and feet... maybe just keep walking.

THE MAN FROM THE PRUDENTIAL (A LOCKED ROOM MURDER, AN IMPOSSIBLE ADDRESS, & THE NAKED MACKINTOSH)

Liverpool 1931

In January 1931, William Herbert Wallace was a man who seemed chemically engineered to be ignored. If you were casting a film about a sensational murder trial, Wallace would be the extra in the background buying a newspaper, not the man in the dock.

He was fifty-two years old. He was soft-spoken. He was neatly dressed in the sort of clothes that suggest respectability but not prosperity. He suffered from a chronic kidney condition that made heavy lifting —or murdering someone with a crowbar—a physical impossibility. He was an insurance agent for the Prudential, a job that involved knocking on doors, collecting pennies, and offering people the grim reassurance that when they died, the paperwork would be in order, and their loved ones provided for.

To his colleagues, he was dependable. To his neighbours, he was invisible. He was the human equivalent of beige wallpaper.

Liverpool in 1931 was a hard city. The depression was biting, the docks were in decline, and the Great War had cast a long, grey shadow over everything. It was a place where respectability was a currency more valuable than gold. For a man like Wallace, life was a series of small, safe boxes: the tram schedule, the insurance ledger, the Sunday suit. He wore a bowler hat. He never raised his voice. He never had a reckless opinion. He was a man who probably apologized to the furniture if he bumped into it.

Wallace lived at 29 Wolverton Street in Anfield. It was a red-brick terrace house in a long line of identical red-brick terrace houses, the architectural embodiment of the lower-middle-class desperate desire to fit in. The parlour faced the street with lace curtains twitching in the window; the scullery was at the back. It was a house built for endurance, not passion.

Inside lived Julia.

If Wallace was beige, Julia Wallace was a splash of colour. She was harder to pin down. She was eccentric, she was said to be sharp-tongued, and she was intensely private. She fancied herself a woman of culture, devoted to music and art in a neighbourhood that cared more about rent and coal. Some neighbours whispered she was older than she claimed, a cardinal sin in 1930s suburbia, whereas others just found her difficult.

The marriage was a curiosity. There were no reports of screaming matches or flying crockery. Instead, it was a "functional" arrangement—two people sharing an address and a teapot, navigating the small corridors of their home like ships passing in a very narrow night. They had no children. They had few visitors. Their evenings were spent in a silence that was either companionable or suffocating, depending on your perspective.

This lack of domestic drama would later become a headache for the police. Murder investigations thrive on noise—on the shouting match heard through the wall, the threat made in the pub. But the Wallaces offered nothing but a vacuum.

Wallace's one escape from the quiet of Wolverton Street was chess. He played at the City Café Chess Club, a modest little organization where men with retreating hairlines and expanding waistlines gathered to exercise their intellects in a world that didn't much value them.

Chess suited Wallace perfectly. It is a game of absolute order. Cause and effect. If you move here, I move there. Nothing is left to chance. There is no luck in chess, only logic. It is a tragedy for Wallace that the rest of his life was about to be dismantled by chaos.

On the evening of Monday, January 19th, 1931, Wallace went to the club. He arrived on time. He sat down. He played. It was the definition of a normal evening, aside from one small details, a short while before his arrival the club had taken an a phone call for Mr Wallace

Since Wallace hadn't yet arrived, the club captain, Mr. Beattie took a message. The caller had a voice that was unremarkable but confident. He identified himself as R.M. Qualtrough.

Whilst the name might sound like a bad cough, or perhaps a Scrabble hand gone wrong, Qualtrough was a relatively common name in Liverpool at the time. It's a Manx name, hailing from the Isle of Mann, a place where hundreds of people in Liverpool had hailed from.

The message left at the chess club was specific. Mr. Qualtrough wished to meet Wallace the following evening to discuss an insurance endowment. The caller was unable to call later due to a family birthday party, but it was good business for Mr Wallace, with the promise of a healthy commission. The appointment was set for 7:30 p.m. The address was 25 Menlove Gardens East.

When Wallace arrived, he was given the message. Now, an insurance agent lives for new leads. It's the thrill of the hunt, or at least, the thrill of the commission. But even then, there were cracks in the facade. Why call a chess club? How did Qualtrough know he would be there? Why an evening meeting? And why Menlove Gardens East?

Wallace, true to form, didn't question it. He pulled out his notebook and wrote the details down. He did it neatly. He did it methodically. Later, prosecutors would wave this notebook around, claiming his lack of hesitation proved he was in on the joke. Defenders would argue it just proved he was a man who followed instructions.

Either way, the trap was set. A message was taken. A man wrote it down. The pieces were on the board.

The next evening, January 20th, Wallace prepared for his appointment. He ate a light supper with Julia. If there was tension in the air, it left no residue. If he was planning to bludgeon her to death later that night, he showed remarkable appetite.

He dressed with his usual fastidious care. Suit pressed. Tie straightened. Bowler hat secured. He looked every inch the Prudential agent.

Julia Wallace was alive when he left. That is the one fact everyone agrees on. He walked out the door at 6:45 p.m., locking it behind him. He walked to the tram stop.

Liverpool in January is not a place for a leisurely stroll.

It is damp, cold, and dark by teatime. Wallace boarded a tram heading south, clutching his notebook with the address: 25 Menlove Gardens East.

Menlove Gardens is a leafy, respectable area, the kind of place where insurance agents dream of retiring. Wallace arrived in good time. He found Menlove Gardens North. He found Menlove Gardens South. He found Menlove Gardens West. He searched for Menlove Gardens East.

It wasn't there.

Now, a normal person might give up after ten minutes. They might assume it was a prank, or a mistake, and head home. But Wallace was not a normal person; he was a bureaucrat. He refused to believe that the map was right and his notebook was wrong.

This is where the evening turned into a farce. Wallace spent the next forty-five minutes conducting the most public alibi tour in history. He didn't just look for the address; he advertised his confusion, making himself as memorable as possible.

He asked a tram conductor. He asked a passer-by. He stopped a policeman. Then another. He visited a newsagent, then stopped another passer-by, and a third policeman. To each of them, he showed his watch. He showed his notebook. He repeated the name. "R.M. Qualtrough. Menlove Gardens East.

He was calm, but perplexed. He was a man trying to solve a logic puzzle that had no solution.

One of the police constables he stopped would later testify that Wallace seemed entirely genuine. He wasn't sweating. He wasn't glancing at a bloodstained cuff. He was just a middle-aged man annoyed that the city planners had apparently forgotten a cardinal direction.

By 8:00 p.m., even Wallace had to admit defeat. There was no Menlove Gardens East. There was no Mr. Qualtrough. There was only the cold Liverpool wind and a wasted tram fare. He turned back. The journey home was slow and uneventful. He sat on the tram, perhaps composing a sternly worded letter to the non-existent Mr. Qualtrough in his head. He arrived back at Wolverton Street shortly before 9:00 p.m.

The house was dark.

Wallace went to the front door. He inserted his key. It wouldn't open. He knocked. He waited. He knocked again.

Next door, the neighbours, Mr. and Mrs. Johnston, were leaving for an evening out. They saw Wallace standing on his step, looking baffled. He turned to them, offering a sentence that would be dissected for decades:

"She won't let me in."

It wasn't said in anger. It was said with the mild confusion of a man whose key had temporarily stopped working.

He tried the front door again. Locked. He walked down the narrow, dark passage to the back of the house. The neighbours watched him go.

He tried the back door. It opened.

Wallace stepped into the darkness of his own kitchen. He called out for Julia. There was no answer. He lit a match, the small flame flickering in the gloom. He walked through the kitchen, into the middle room, and finally, into the front parlour.

What he found there would shatter the beige monotony of his life forever.

Julia was lying on the floor. The room, usually so pristine, was a scene of carnage. She had been beaten to death with a violence that defied belief.

Wallace didn't scream. He didn't run into the street tearing his hair out. He walked back out to the neighbours, pale but composed, and calmly asked them to fetch the police. When the officers arrived, they found a man who was helpful, polite, and deeply shaken. But to the cynical eyes of the Liverpool police, he wasn't shaken enough. He wasn't weeping. He wasn't hysterical. He was just... Wallace.

And in the eyes of the law, being quiet is often the most suspicious thing a man can do.

From the moment the detectives opened their notebooks, the "Menlove Gardens" excursion started to look less like a bad day and more like a bad script.

Suspicion didn't just attach itself to Wallace's journey; it clung to it. The very thing that made his alibi so robust—the sheer number of people he annoyed while asking for directions—was also what made it so suspicious.

Think about it. If you are innocent and looking for an address, you ask a question, you get an answer, you move on. Wallace didn't just ask; he performed. He stopped tram conductors. He stopped policemen. He stopped random citizens. He checked his watch with theatrical precision. He practically handed out business cards saying, "Hello, I am currently not murdering my wife."

The police were left with a headache. On one hand, Wallace's movements were traced with a clarity that is almost unheard of in 1931. We know where he was at 7:06 p.m. We know where he was at 7:15 p.m. But on the other hand, the logic was twisted. If you want to disappear to commit a crime, you don't spend an hour making sure every tram conductor in Liverpool remembers your face.

Unless, of course, that was the point.

Back at Wolverton Street, the police were dealing with a different kind of physics problem. The parlour was a slaughterhouse. Julia Wallace hadn't just been killed; she had been obliterated. The killer had used a blunt instrument—likely an iron bar or a heavy poker—and struck her with a ferocity that sprayed blood across the walls, the furniture, and the floor. It was a crime of rage, intimate and messy.

And standing right in the middle of it was William Herbert Wallace, looking like he'd just come back from dry cleaning his soul. He was immaculate. His suit was clean. His shirt cuffs were white. His hands were spotless. His hair was combed.

This was the paradox that would haunt the prosecution. To beat a woman to death in a small room requires energy and proximity. The laws of fluid dynamics suggest that the killer should have been covered in gore. Yet Wallace looked ready for Sunday service.

He answered their questions with that maddening, detached calm. He explained the locked front door. He explained the open back door. He explained the missing cash box (four pounds gone—hardly the heist of the century). To some officers, he looked like a man in shock. To most, however, he looked like a man who had rehearsed his lines in the mirror.

The house was searched. It wasn't ransacked. The "robbery" theory looked flimsy. Burglars rarely break in, ignore the valuables, beat a woman to death, steal four quid, and leave without knocking over a single chair.

And then, under the body of the victim, they found the coat. It was an old mackintosh, belonging to Wallace. It was partially burned, as if someone had tried to set fire to it and then given up, or perhaps used it to smother a small flame.

For the police, this sodden, singed raincoat was the Rosetta Stone. It allowed them to construct a theory so wild, so grotesque, and yet so oddly compelling that it became the defining image of the case.

They reasoned as follows: How does a man kill his wife without getting blood on his suit? Simple. He takes the suit off.

Thus, the "Naked Mackintosh" theory was born. The prosecution suggested that Wallace had stripped naked (or perhaps down to his underwear), donned the raincoat, beaten his wife to death, washed his hands, dressed back into his pristine suit, and then—in a moment of baffling incompetence—left the bloody raincoat under the dead body and tried to burn it.

It was a theory that required Wallace to be two different people at once.

Person A was a criminal mastermind, a "chess player" capable of plotting a complex fake alibi involving a non-existent address and a telephone call to a club.

Person B was a complete idiot who leaves the murder weapon's camouflage under the victim and tries to light a fire in a room full of blood.

The theory also demanded a physical feat that would have exhausted a man in his prime, let alone a fifty-two-year-old man with failing kidneys. He had to kill, clean up, dress, and run for a tram, all within a window of time that was shrinking by the minute.

The police worked backward. They decided Wallace never went to Menlove Gardens first. They theorized he came home, killed Julia, and then went on his magical mystery tour to establish the alibi.

But for that to be the case, the timeline was tight, with no room for error..

Witnesses placed Julia alive at 6:30 p.m. (she spoke to a milk boy). Wallace was on a tram at 7:06 p.m. That gave him roughly 30 minutes to argue with his wife, strip naked, put on a raincoat, bludgeon her to death, wash himself scrupulously clean, dress, fake a robbery, try to burn the coat, fail to burn the coat, and walk to the tram stop without looking flushed or out of breath.

It was the sort of schedule that would make a frantic commuter weep. And yet, the police believed it. Ultimately, they had to. Because if they didn't believe it, they had no suspect.

They staged a re-enactment, proving that it could be done, using a young officer. A young officer who was left exhausted by the feat, which should have ruled Wallace out given his ailing health, but that didn't matter.

The press, naturally, loved it. The "Naked Mackintosh Murder." It had a ring to it. It conjured up an image that was both terrifying and ridiculous—the mild-mannered insurance agent transforming into a plastic-clad butcher.

Wallace was arrested and charged.

But Wallace wasn't just a man standing alone; he was a life long Company Man. And the Prudential Assurance

Company didn't take kindly to the idea that one of their agents—the very face of steady, boring reliability—was a hatchet-wielding maniac. It was bad for the brand. People buy insurance to protect against disaster, not to invite it into the parlour for tea. So, the Union stepped in, and the corporate war chest was cracked open. They didn't just hire a defence team; they bought a rehearsal.

In a move that feels less like 1930s Liverpool and more like a modern legal thriller, the defence supposedly didn't leave anything to chance. The story goes that they staged elaborate mock trials behind closed doors, recruiting legal minds to play the judge and finding stand-ins for the jury. They ran Wallace through the wringer, testing the timeline, poking holes in the "Naked Mackintosh" theory, and polishing his answers until they shone with the dull lustre of absolute truth.

By the time William Wallace stepped into the real court, he wasn't just testifying; he was performing a role that had been focus-grouped, funded, and rehearsed by one of the richest companies in Britain. Justice might be blind, but it helps if you can afford to buy her a new pair of glasses.

At the trial, the prosecution leaned hard on the "Chess Player" angle. They painted Wallace not as a boring man, but as a cold, calculating strategist. They argued that the fake phone call (from "R.M. Qualtrough") was made by Wallace himself the night before, disguising his voice, to set up the game. The Menlove Gardens trip wasn't a mistake; it was a masterpiece of misdirection.

When the police traced the origin of the call, the line didn't lead to a business district or a distant suburb. It led to a public telephone kiosk at the corner of Rochester Road and Breck Road. That is a mere four hundred yards from the Wallace home, around a three-minute walk, even for someone in as ill health as Wallace. It was close enough to see the chimney of number 29.

This proximity turned the phone box into a smoking gun. In the prosecution's eyes, it was Wallace himself, slipping out of his house, walking to the box, placing the call to the club to set up his own alibi, and then strolling on to the café to act the part of the surprised recipient.

Then there is the matter of the voice. Samuel Beattie, the club captain who took the message, described "Qualtrough" as having a confident, strong voice. Yet the exchange operators who connected the line described a different tone entirely, something muffled, indistinct, perhaps a voice trying to hide itself. It leaves us with the unsettling image of a man pressing a handkerchief over the mouthpiece, breathing the damp Liverpool air, and speaking a name that would send a woman to her grave.

A brazen act of ventriloquism performed almost on his own doorstep.

The defence, led by Roland Oliver, looked at the jury and essentially asked: Really? In their dummy trials this had worked a charm.

They pointed out the absurdity. If this was a plan, it was the worst plan in history. Why choose an address that didn't exist? That only guarantees you will be remembered. Why involve the chess club? Why leave the coat? Why burn the coat?

If Wallace was a genius, why did he essentially frame himself? And if he was a bungler, how did he manage the "impossible" clean-up?

And going back to the phone call, they argued that

if Wallace was innocent, the alternative was arguably worse. It meant the caller was a watcher. It suggested a man standing in the illuminated red box, receiver in hand, looking down the street at the Wallace home, waiting for the husband to be safely ensconced at his chess game so the trap could be laid for the following night.

As the trial moved forward, the parlour at 29 Wolverton Street sat silent and empty. The blood was scrubbed away, but the questions remained.

By the time the jury was sent out to deliberate, one thing was clear. The case against Wallace wasn't built on hard evidence. It wasn't built on any evidence at all. It was built on a story. A story about a man who could be two things at once: a boring husband and a naked monster.

And juries, as we know, love a good story.

The jury at the Liverpool Assizes that day were not in the mood for nuance. They deliberated for just one hour and their verdict: Guilty.

William Herbert Wallace was sentenced to hang by the neck until dead. The men from the Pru were in shock but to the wider world, for a moment at least, the world made sense. The husband did it. The husband always does it. Order was restored. But almost immediately, the "victory" felt hollow. The public, the press, and even legal scholars looked at the verdict and then looked at the evidence, and realized the two didn't match.

Then, something happened that almost never happens in the British legal system.

Wallace appealed. The Court of Criminal Appeal in London reviewed the case. Usually, appeals are won on technicalities, a judge gave the wrong instruction, or a piece of evidence was inadmissible. Not this time.

The judges looked at the prosecution's story, the naked mackintosh, the impossible timeline, the phantom phone call, and essentially said: "This is nonsense."

They overturned the conviction on the grounds that the verdict was not supported by the evidence. It was a legal bombshell. It was the first time in British history a murder conviction was quashed simply because the jury had gotten it wrong.

William Wallace walked out of prison a free man. The Prudential had, to their eyes, insured justice for one of their own.

Freedom, however, is a relative term. Wallace was legally innocent, but socially radioactive. He returned to his job, but clients wouldn't open the door to him. People crossed the street to avoid him. He wasn't just an insurance agent any more; he was, to parts of Liverpool at least, The Man Who Got Away With It.

The police, stung by the humiliation in court, had no appetite to reopen the case. If Wallace didn't do it, someone else must have, but they'd sooner forget the whole thing.

Briefly, eyes turned to a man named Richard Gordon Parry. Parry was a junior insurance agent who knew Wallace. He had a criminal record. He was known to use aliases. He knew where the cash box was kept. And, most damningly, he was even known to sometimes use the name "Qualtrough."

It seemed perfect. But the police, perhaps too exhausted or too embarrassed, let the momentum die. Parry was never charged. The file was closed, but the case remained an open wound.

Wallace tried to rebuild his life, but the stress ate him alive. His fragile kidneys finally gave out. In 1933, just two years after walking free, he died, his failing health finally catching up with him. He went to his grave insisting that R.M. Qualtrough was real.

The case has haunted crime writers for nearly a century. Raymond Chandler called it "the non-pareil of all murder mysteries," a case so perfectly balanced between guilt and innocence that it feels designed by a novelist.

Was Wallace an innocent man destroyed by a cosmic coincidence? Was he a genius who concocted a plan so bizarre that no one could prove it? Or was the truth just messy, stupid, and accidental?

We are left with a crime scene that makes no sense, a man who acted like a robot, and a street that never existed. Menlove Gardens East is not on any map, but it is permanently etched into the folklore of Liverpool.

Somewhere, in a chess club that no longer exists, a phone is ringing. A message is being taken. And a life is being dismantled by a lie.

There is, finally, one last theory. It is a theory that sits in the dark corner of the room, uninvited but impossible to ignore.

It accepts the physical reality: Wallace was too old, too sick, and too weak to beat his wife to death and clean up the mess in under twenty minutes. But it rejects the idea that he was an innocent victim. It suggests something colder.

The biggest problem in the Wallace case has always been the blood. Julia was brutally beaten. The room was painted in gore. Wallace was spotless.

So, what if he never lifted a hand? What if he simply moved the pieces?

This is the "Murder by Proxy" theory. It suggests that Wallace wasn't the executioner; he was the architect. It's a theory that wasn't explored back in the 1930s but, to this author, it has a certain allure.

Wallace was a chess player. Chess players generally don't rush. They sacrifice pawns. They control the board from a distance.

Consider this: Wallace walked the streets of Liverpool every day. He knew who was desperate. He knew who owed money. He knew who would do anything for a few pounds. In 1931, Liverpool was a city on its knees. Men were starving. Desperation makes for cheap labour, even in murder, and it's well within the realms of possibility that Wallace had an untraceable "rainy day" fund to

He sets the board, stages the phone call to the chess club, to give his hired hand a window of opportunity. Then the night of the murder he set about creating the most public alibi in history. He ensures that every tram conductor, policeman, and passer-by in South Liverpool sees him looking for an imaginary address. He makes himself the most visible man in the city at the exact moment the crime is taking place.

Meanwhile, the "Pawn" enters the house. Maybe Julia lets him in; there was no forced entry. Maybe she knows him.

The violence happens. It is messy. It is brutal. But it is not Wallace's problem. He is miles away, checking his watch, waiting for the endgame.

If this theory is true, then the image of Wallace on the

tram becomes the most chilling part of the story. He isn't a confused husband. He is a man sitting calmly in a moving theatre, waiting for his wife to die.

But even this theory hits a wall. Money. The only thing missing was four pounds. Even in the Depression, that's a low fee for a hit. Unless Wallace paid upfront. Unless the killer panicked. Unless the plan went wrong.

Perhaps the "Pawn" botched it. Perhaps he left the weapon. Perhaps he panicked and shoved Wallace's own mackintosh under the body, framing the very man who hired him.

Imagine Wallace coming home. He expects a clean scene. Instead, he finds carnage and his own coat soaking in the evidence.

If that is the truth, then Wallace wasn't a genius, and he wasn't innocent. He was just a man who thought he could control the game, only to realize that murder doesn't follow the rules of chess. More often than not it follows the rules of chaos instead.

But as always, we hit the same brick wall. There is no proof. Although, the phone call to the chess club, when looked at in a different light, does offer some circumstantial evidence. It also explains why the call was so memorable to the telephone operators.

The caller did something that suggests a specific type of personality. When the call initially failed to connect, he demanded to speak to the manager.

He called back the exchange. He complained. He was fussy, insistent, and bureaucratic. He told the operator that he had pressed Button A but had not received his connection. He demanded the operator put him through manually to the café to ensure the call was completed.

This act of petty officiousness was either a fatal mistake or a stroke of genius. By complaining, the caller ensured he wasn't just a faceless voice in the wire; he became a problem. He annoyed the operators. He forced them to interact with him, to remember his tone, and, crucially, to log the fault.

It created a paper trail where there shouldn't have been one. Because of that complaint, we know the exact time of the call. We know the operators remembered him. It fits the profile of William Wallace perfectly, a man who lived by the rulebook and hated to be short-changed.

But it also fits the profile of a killer desperate to ensure that the message was received, logged, and stamped into history. It gave Qualtrough a paper trail. If this is the case perhaps Wallace thought that the complaint log would prove it wasn't him? Naively not realising that, even a century ago, a phone call could easily be traced.

The Puppet Master theory explains the bloodless suit. It explains the alibi. It can even explain the voice on the phone call. But ultimately, relying solely on loose circumstantial evidence, it explains nothing.

And so, the case ends where it began: in the fog.

William Wallace is dead. Julia Wallace is dead. And the truth lies buried somewhere between Menlove Gardens East and Menlove Gardens West—in the space where the map runs out.

Perhaps that is the only verdict we can give. Not "Guilty," not "Not Guilty." Just...

Stalemate, rather than Checkmate.

THE FIELD OF THE DEAD (OR, MANCHESTER'S DIRTY SECRET)

Manchester, 19th Century

Manchester likes to think of itself as the engine room of the modern world. Cotton. Canals. Chimneys scraping the sky. The city where the future was forged in smoke and sweat. But progress has a price tag, and usually, it's the poor who foot the bill.

If you step off the train at Victoria Station and walk north, you might find yourself in a place called Angel Meadow. It sounds delightful, doesn't it? A place for picnics, daisies, and poets.

In reality, by the mid-19th century, Angel Meadow was "hell upon earth," those were the words of philosopher Friedrich Engels. It was one of the most densely populated slums in Europe, tucked between the cathedral and the polluted sludge of the River Irk.

Thirty thousand people were crammed into rotting terraces built on top of a burial ground. Yes, you read that right. The dead never left. They just got new neighbours.

Angel Meadow was the sort of place where people disappeared not with a bang, not even with a whimper, they simply wandered off and vanished. Lodgers died in their sleep and were carted away before breakfast. Women entered the workhouse and left without their babies, if they left at all.

In 1849, workmen digging foundations for new housing uncovered a horror show. Skulls. Femurs. Coffins crushed flat by the weight of the city. Officially, these were old burials. Unofficially? The locals knew better. Some of the bones had no coffin marks. Some showed signs of blunt force trauma. One skull had a fracture so severe it couldn't have come from settling earth.

The city shrugged. Manchester had mills to run. The Industrial Revolution didn't stop for skeletons. The pragmatic solution? Build over them.

But the darkest thread wasn't the bones; it was the babies. In Angel Meadow, life was cheap, and new life was cheapest of all. Unmarried mothers, desperate and shamed, paid "baby farmers" to take their infants off their hands. No questions asked. No receipts given. Some babies were fostered. Many were not.

Bodies of infants were found in privies, cellars, and walled up in chimneys. It was a massacre of the innocent, conducted quietly behind closed doors. Who killed them? Officially, no one. Unofficially, poverty held the pillow.

And then there were the adults. In 1867 alone, police records list over 200 "sudden or unexplained" deaths in the area. A man beaten for gin money. A woman was strangled in a lodging house. A drunk falling into the Irk and not coming back up.

No serial killer. No mastermind. Just relentless, grinding violence made mundane by misery. Angel Meadow didn't need a murderer; it was one.

If Angel Meadow had a signature crime scene, it wasn't a dark alley; it was the River Irk, which was less a waterway, and more an open sewer, thick with dye, waste, and bodies. On a damp morning in the autumn of 1848, a body was pulled from the sludge.

The official paperwork is frustratingly thin. A brief notice in the paper. A coroner's scribble. She was described simply as "A young woman, believed to be between sixteen and twenty years of age, found drowned."

That's it. No name. No address. No occupation. Just "young."

But the coroner noticed details, even if he didn't act on them. Her hands were rough—factory work. Her dress was patched and oversized—charity clothes. She had no bonnet—the Victorian shorthand for destitution or madness. And she had bruises. Bruises on her arms that suggested she had been grabbed. Bruises that suggested a struggle.

In true Victorian fashion, the inquest wasn't held in a court; it was held in a pub. Twelve men were sworn in as jurors—tradesmen, labourers, men who had likely already had a pint or three. The coroner asked his questions. A doctor shrugged. A constable nodded.

Did anyone know her? No.

Did anyone see her fall? No.

In a district where people slept four or more to a bed and moved every week, anonymity was the norm.

The jury returned a verdict: "Found Drowned."

Not murder. Not manslaughter. The river did it.

What is striking is the silence. No one asked where she slept. No one asked who she was with. No one asked why a young girl was alone by the Irk after dark. They didn't ask because they already knew the answer. In

Angel Meadow, after dark, the rules changed. Violence became casual. If a woman ended up in the river, the assumption was simple: she made a bad choice.

The coroner closed the book. The girl was buried in a pauper's grave, layered into soil already dense with the forgotten. If she had a name, it wasn't recorded. If she had dreams, they died in the water.

By the late 19th century, Angel Meadow began to vanish. Slum clearances tore through the terraces. The streets were renamed. The burial ground was paved over (again) and Manchester moved on.

Today, if you stand near Victoria Station, you are standing on top of Angel Meadow. Trams rattle past. Commuters eat sandwiches. Tourists take selfies by the cathedral.

Nothing looks haunted. And that is the clever part. Angel Meadow doesn't shout. Its horror is quiet, structural, and buried deep beneath the pavement.

So, what is the unsolved mystery of Angel Meadow? It isn't "Who killed the girl in the river?" We will never know that. The mystery is: How many were there? How long was it allowed to happen? How did an entire district become a death zone without anyone blinking?

The girl in the Irk has no name. But she has a story.

She represents the "acceptable losses" of the Victorian age. If she had been middle class, her bruises would have raised an alarm. If she had lived in a nice suburb, her death would have been a scandal.

Instead, she was poor. She was female. She was in Angel Meadow. And that made her invisible.

Today, the river is culverted. The slums are gone. But if you listen carefully over the noise of the traffic, you can almost hear the deafening silence where the questions should have been asked.

Manchester walks over her story every single day. And the saddest part is, it doesn't even know she's there.

THE PUSHER (OR, HISTORY REPEATING DOWN BY THE IRK)

Manchester, Present Day?

Every city has a stretch of water that attracts rumours like flies to a spilled pint. In Manchester, as we have seen, that water is the Irk. And the canals that feed it.

Long before the internet coined the hashtag "The Manchester Pusher," Angel Meadow had already built a reputation as a place where people checked out of the vertical world and into the horizontal one via the water. They didn't go dramatically. They didn't go memorably. They just went quietly, inconveniently, and often without a splash.

In the nineteenth century, bodies were hooked out of the Irk with such regularity that it barely made the ink dry on the morning papers. The phrase "Found Drowned" appears in the coroner's records with a chilling frequency. It was a shorthand verdict. A bureaucratic shrug. It neatly avoided questions of blame, responsibility, or further paperwork.

Men fell in drunk. Women slipped in despair. Children wandered too close. That was the official line. The Victorian Boogeyman

And yet, even then, the city whispered.

The Victorians didn't have the vocabulary we have now. The term "serial killer" wouldn't be popularised until the 1980s. They didn't have psychological profiling or podcast sleuths.

But they absolutely believed in men who haunted rivers.

If you read the column inches closely, you find hints. Unnamed figures loitering near the towpaths. Shadows seen moving just before a splash. Arguments heard in the fog but never described in detail.

Lodging-house gossip was far less restrained than the broadsheets. There were stories of men who befriended the desperate, bought them a gin, walked them toward the water's edge, and walked back alone.

Nothing provable. Nothing you could put in a charge sheet. Just rumours that persisted.

If there was someone hunting the night then Angel Meadow was the perfect hunting ground. It was crowded, anonymous, and transient. If someone disappeared into the murk of the Irk, the city simply stepped over the gap they left and carried on.

Fast forward to the 2010s. The slums are now long gone, they've been replaced by glass apartments and trendy bars. But the rumours? They just held their breath for a century, and then suddenly, the stories surfaced again.

Young men found drowned in canals. Late-night walks home. No witnesses. No clear signs of a struggle.

The press gave it a name, The Manchester Pusher, because naming a monster makes it feel small enough to fight. Online forums lit up with maps, timelines, and theories. Amateur detectives sat in bedrooms hundreds of miles away, circling towpaths in red digital ink, connecting dots that they claimed the police refused to see.

And suddenly, the old stories about Angel Meadow didn't feel so old. They felt uncomfortably familiar. The questions were the same, just dressed in modern clothes:

* Why here?

* Why so often?

* Why always at night?

* Why did no one ever see the moment of the fall? In the 1800s that was a lack of human witnesses. 150 years later it was a distinct lack of CCTV footage. In a city covered in cameras it was decidedly odd.

The police, understandably, poured cold water on the idea. They cited the dangers of too much alcohol. They cited gravity. They cited the treacherous nature of unlit towpaths and the tragedy of coincidence.

Which is, almost word for word, what their Victorian predecessors.

The river and the canal offer the perfect accomplice. Water erases evidence. It washes away fingerprints and fibres. It softens the timeline of death. It confuses injuries—was that bruise from a fist, or from hitting a lock gate on the way down?

Most importantly, water gives authority figures an easy answer when nobody is demanding a difficult one.

In Victorian Angel Meadow, drowned bodies belonged to the poor, the desperate, and the invisible. In the modern city, they usually belong to young men out late, alone, and assumed to be drunk.

Different centuries. Same assumption: They brought it on themselves.

Folklore around the Irk still carries the older DNA of the rumour. Some locals will tell you the river is cursed. Others say it attracts bad luck. A few will lean in over a pint and say, quietly, that it attracts bad people.

And then there are the cynics—the ones who point out that you don't need ghosts or serial killers. You just need darkness, isolation, and a city council that doesn't put up enough railings.

But that belief has survived remarkably well. If Angel Meadow is haunted—and many would swear it is—it isn't by a single ghost in a sheet.

It is haunted by repetition.

It is haunted by the same explanations recycled every generation. By the same shrugging verdicts. By the same reluctance to join the dots because the picture they make is too ugly to contemplate.

Whether the "Manchester Pusher" exists as a flesh-and-blood killer is, in some ways, beside the point. What matters is that the story feels plausible. It feels true because the city has spent two hundred years proving that people can disappear into its waterways without too much fuss.

The River Irk has always been very good at keeping secrets. And Manchester has always been very good at letting it.

Stand by the water today. It's hard to reconcile the tidy paths and the geese with the weight of history. The slums are gone. The lodging houses are dust. The bones are buried deep.

But the rumours persist.

Because rivers remember, even when cities pretend not to. And somewhere between the Victorian dead of Angel Meadow and the modern headlines, lies an uncomfortable truth:

Some stories don't die. They just tread water, waiting for a new generation to tell them again.

The Irk is still flowing. And it is still waiting.

The truly terrifying possibility then isn't that there is a Pusher, it's rather that if there is one, the authorities wouldn't notice until it's far too late.

THE VIEW FROM THE CARRIAGE (OR, MURDER IN PASSING)

Leeds, 1968

In the late 1960s, Leeds was a city having a nervous breakdown.

The post-war optimism had curdled into something greyer and grittier. The bomb sites had been cleared, but in their place rose the concrete monoliths of the future—brutalist architecture that promised modernity but mostly delivered wind tunnels and anonymity. The last vestiges of the Victorian slums were being bulldozed, communities were being scattered to the winds, and the city felt like it was stuck in a cold, damp limbo between the past and the future.

It was a city in transition. And as any copper will tell you, transition is just a fancy word for "a good time to get away with murder."

On the night of February 26, 1968, the winter had Leeds in a choke-hold. The pavements were slick with ice, the air was brittle, and the only things moving with any purpose were the trains cutting through the city centre. The railway was the city's artery—pumping commuters, drunks, and insomniacs through the heart of the darkness.

Near the Parish Church, by Kirkgate, lay a patch of waste ground. It was a scar on the landscape, a piece of land the developers hadn't quite figured out how to monetize. It was dark, it was quiet, and it was the kind of place you only went if you had nowhere else to be.

That night, Mary Judge walked into that darkness. She wouldn't walk out.

Mary was forty-two years old. To the social workers, she was a case file. To the police, she was a "known associate" of the pavement. In the polite, sterile language of the 1960s officialdom, she was described as being "of unsettled circumstances."

In reality, this meant she was homeless, vulnerable, and largely invisible. She lived on the margins, moving between pubs and shelters, known by face but rarely by name. She was one of the city's forgotten, tolerated when she had the money for a drink, dismissed when she didn't.

Earlier that evening, Mary had been doing what many of us would do on a freezing night in Leeds: finding a radiator and a drink. She was seen in the pubs around Kirkgate, wrapped up against the biting wind. There was nothing unusual about her. She was just part of the furniture.

Sometime after midnight, the alcohol or the closing times pushed her out of the light and towards the waste ground opposite the church. What happened next is the stuff of nightmares, not because of what we know, but because of how we know it.

Usually, murders are witnessed by people standing nearby. They hear a scream; they see a struggle. The murder of Mary Judge was different. It was witnessed at forty miles per hour.

As a train roared out of Leeds station, high on the viaducts, its headlights swept across the waste ground like a lighthouse beam cutting through fog. Inside one of the carriages, a young boy was looking out of the window, perhaps bored, perhaps just watching the city slide by.

For a split second—a heartbeat—the darkness was illuminated.

The boy saw a tableau frozen in the strobe light of the train. He saw a woman on the ground. He saw a man standing over her, bent at the waist, striking her repeatedly.

The boy later described the attacker: tall, slim, long dark hair. And then, whoosh. The train passed. The light vanished. The darkness snapped back shut like a coffin lid.

It is a terrifying concept. A brutal murder framed for a single second by the lights of a passing train. The boy couldn't stop the train. He couldn't scream a warning. He was like a spectator in a cinema, watching a horror movie, one he couldn't pause.

The boy, to his credit, reported what he'd seen as soon as he left the train and Mary Judge was found soon after. The violence inflicted on her was absolute.

She had been beaten with such ferocious intensity that her face was unrecognizable. She was found naked from the waist down, her clothing scattered nearby like debris. The police officers who arrived at the scene, men who had likely seen their fair share of bar brawls and domestic disputes, were shaken. This wasn't a robbery gone wrong; this was rage.

Because her face was injured beyond recognition, the police had to identify her by her fingerprints. It was the only dignity left to give her. The investigation began, but it was hobbled from the start by the calendar. It was

1968.

They didn't have DNA profiling, they didn't have CCTV on every corner, and there was no mobile phone triangulation. Forensic science was largely a guy in a white coat looking at things through a magnifying glass whilst smoking a pipe.

The killer had left no fingerprints (or at least, none that could be found in the mud and grime). There was no blood trail that offered a specific type. There was just a body and a description from a boy on a moving train.

The detectives did what they could. They hit the pavements of Kirkgate. They bullied information out of bar staff, taxi drivers, and the local drinkers.

They found a man who had been drinking with Mary earlier that night. He was arrested. He was questioned. He was sweated in a cell. But eventually, he was released. There was no physical evidence linking him to the crime, and no witness could place him on the waste ground at the critical moment.

The boy's description, Tall, Slim, Dark Hair, applied to half the male population under thirty in Leeds at the time. It was like looking for a needle in a stack of needles.

As the days turned into weeks, the case grew cold. The newspapers, initially interested in the gore, moved on to newer scandals. Mary Judge's file began its slow migration to the bottom of the stack. She was another unsolved statistic in a city that was too busy knocking down buildings to care about the people living in their rubble.

Years later, the case of Mary Judge would be dragged back into the light, but for all the wrong reasons.

In the 1970s, West Yorkshire became the hunting ground for the Yorkshire Ripper, Peter Sutcliffe. As the body count rose, the police began to panic. They looked back through the archives, desperate to find the start of the pattern. Mary Judge's murder ticked a lot of the boxes.

* The Victim: A woman on the margins.

* The Method: Brutal, blunt-force trauma to the head.

* The Location: A bleak, industrial waste ground.

For a while, the public and the press were convinced Mary was an early, uncredited victim of the Ripper. It makes for a tidy narrative. It connects the dots. Humans love patterns; we hate chaos.

But the police, and later the forensic reviews, said no. Sutcliffe's modus operandi was different in the details. The forensics didn't match. Officially, they declared, Mary Judge was not a Ripper victim.

But if that is the case it leaves us with something almost more unsettling.

If it wasn't one of the most famous monsters in British history, then who was it? It meant there was another man in Leeds capable of beating a woman to death in the shadow of a church, who simply walked away and never did it again—or, worse, did it again and never got caught.

The waste ground is gone now, buried under the redevelopment that finally finished what the 1960s had started. The physical memory of the crime has been erased by concrete and commerce.

But the human memory remains.

The boy on the train grew up. In later life, he spoke

of that night, the cold glass against his forehead, the sudden flash of light, and the image that burned itself into his retina. He carried the weight of being the only person to see Mary Judge's final moments, a helpless audience of one, for the rest of his life. There wasn't a word for it at the time, but it's clear he suffered PTSD.

Mary Judge wasn't a symbol of urban decay, and she wasn't a footnote in the Ripper story. She was a woman who was failed twice: first by a society that left her to freeze on the streets, and second by a justice system that couldn't name her killer.

Her killer hasn't been found. To date there have been no deathbed confessions. Given the passage of time, her death was almost 60 years ago, it's likely too late for justice.

The case of the Woman by the Tracks remains a grim reminder of the lottery of justice. Sometimes, the evidence is overwhelming. And sometimes, life is just a train rushing through the dark. You see the horror for a split second, and then it's gone.

THE DRAPER'S LAST CUSTOMER (OR, MURDER BY THE YARD)

Sheffield, 1945

On the morning of Saturday, January 13, 1945, Sheffield was a city holding its breath.

The war was stumbling toward its conclusion, but it wasn't over yet. The Luftwaffe had done their worst to the city's steel heart years earlier, leaving gaps in the streets like missing teeth. But Sheffield carried on. Trams rattled down the streets, blackout paint peeled from the windows, and people queued for their rations with the grim determination that only Yorkshire folk can muster.

Ecclesall Road was awake. It was the artery of the south-west, a bustle of coats, errands, and the crackle of gossip.

At number 72 stood a narrow drapery shop, selling buttons, needles, and the sort of sensible fabric that won the war. Eleanor Charlotte Hammerton ran it. She was a woman in her seventies who lived alone above the shop. Her life was measured in yards of cotton and small change. She was a fixture. A part of the scenery.

That morning, however, Eleanor Hammerton was dead.

She was found inside her own shop, lying amidst the scattered bolts of cloth and overturned stock. She hadn't just died; she had been severely beaten. The violence inflicted on this elderly woman was so severe, so personal, that it turned the cosy domesticity of the drapery into a battlefield.

There were no witnesses. There were no suspects. And despite the murder happening on one of the busiest roads in the city, in broad daylight no less, the killer simply walked away.

To understand why this case remains unsolved, you have to understand 1945.

We tend to look back at the war years with a rose-tinted nostalgia—everyone pulling together, Mrs. Miniver, cups of tea in the shelter. But the reality was messier. Sheffield was a city of transients. You had demobilized soldiers trying to remember how to be civilians. You had refugees. You had munitions workers. You had people whose homes had been flattened, moving from lodging to lodging.

It was a time when "mind your own business" wasn't just advice; it was a survival strategy.

Eleanor Hammerton was the perfect victim for such a time. She lived alone. She had no close family looking out for her. She didn't keep detailed accounts (because why would you, when the taxman has bigger problems?).

When the police arrived, they found a scene of chaos. Eleanor had been beaten about the head. The ferocity suggested panic or rage. A professional burglar hits you once and leaves. A maniac hits you until you stop moving.

The police did the usual math: Dead Shopkeeper + Messy Shop = Robbery. It's a logical assumption. But logic is often the first casualty of a murder investigation.

If it was a robbery, it was a terrible one. Eleanor wasn't wealthy. She ran a drapery shop in the middle of a war; she wasn't keeping the Crown Jewels in the biscuit tin. Cash records were vague, so nobody knew exactly what, if anything, was taken.

And then there is the "Ecclesall Road Problem." This wasn't a dark alley. This was a main road. There were trams. There were shoppers. There were nosy neighbours. For a killer to enter the shop, beat an old woman to death, rummage through the stock, and then leave without a single person seeing anything suspicious, requires a level of luck that borders on the supernatural.

Unless, of course, the killer didn't look suspicious. Was it a customer? A delivery boy? A neighbour? Someone who could walk out with blood on their cuff and simply blend into the grey, exhausted crowd?

The most tragic part of the Hammerton case is the silence. Eleanor left no diaries. She left no letters hinting at a feud. She was a private woman who lived a quiet, private, life. As a result, she remains a mystery. Today, we only know from her autopsy report.

This was the fate of many elderly women in the mid-20th century. They existed in the background of society, essential, but invisible. When violence visited them, it was treated as a freak weather event, shocking but inexplicable.

The police did their best. They canvassed the street. They knocked on doors. They chased rumours of "strange men" and "shifty soldiers." But in 1945, half the men in the country looked shifty and tired.

They couldn't even pin down the time of death

accurately. Had she opened the shop? Was the killer waiting for her? Was the "Closed" sign turned to "Open"? The timeline was as foggy as a November morning.

We look back at these cases and scream at the history books: Check the DNA! Check the CCTV!

But in 1945, the police toolkit was basically a notebook, a whistle, and a stern look. Fingerprinting was only useful if you had a suspect to match it to. Blood analysis could tell you "It's human," but not "It's Dave from down the road."

Without a witness and without a confession, the police were helpless. The investigation stalled. The file grew thinner. The war in Europe ended in May, and the murder of one old lady in Sheffield was swallowed up by the jubilant roar of Victory in Europe.

The shop at number 72 was cleaned up. The blood was scrubbed from the floorboards. The stock was sold or thrown away. The shop changed hands, then changed hands again.

Today, Ecclesall Road is a hipster's paradise of coffee shops, bars, and student flats. Thousands of people walk past number 72 every day. They stare at their phones, they laugh with their friends, and they have absolutely no idea that they are walking through a crime scene.

There is no blue plaque for Eleanor. There is no memorial.

The Hammerton murder isn't famous because it changed the world. It's famous, to the few who know it, because it is so profoundly, depressingly unfinished. It reminds us that safety is an illusion. Eleanor survived the Blitz. She survived the shortages. She survived the fear of invasion. She survived The First World War and the Spanish Flu Pandemic.

She just didn't survive a Saturday morning at work.

And in a country that prides itself on "Keep Calm and Carry On," this is the dark side of that motto. We carried on. We rebuilt. We moved forward.

But in doing so we left Eleanor behind.

THE BONFIRE OF IDENTITY (OR, THE MAN WHO WASN'T THERE)

Birmingham, 1978

On May 12, 1978, a man named William Norman Simpson died in Birmingham. He was forty-five years old. And that is where the facts stop and the fog begins.

Usually, when you pull on the thread of a murder case, you find a tangle of knots: witnesses, motives, grieving relatives, grainy newsprint photos. But with William Norman Simpson, the thread just snaps in your hand.

He was shot. Then, for good measure, his body was set on fire. Now, in the world of murder, this is not a subtle act. A poisoning is quiet. A stabbing is intimate. But shooting a man and then setting him alight is a spectacle. It is an act that screams for attention. It demands headlines. It demands a manhunt.

Yet, Birmingham didn't blink. The city absorbed the violence, shrugged its concrete shoulders, and carried on. There are no newspaper splashes to be found in the archives. There is no folklore. There is no Wikipedia page debating the ballistics.

William Norman Simpson left behind no ghost, only a patch of scorched earth and a silence so loud it hurts your ears to listen to it.

To understand how a man can be gunned down and torched without anyone really noticing, you have to understand Birmingham in 1978.

This wasn't the polished, regenerated city of today with its shiny Bullring and canal-side bistros. This was a city on its knees. The manufacturing heart of Britain was suffering from cardiac arrest. Jobs were vanishing, strikes were paralysing the streets, and the IRA bombing campaign had left nerves shattered.

It was a grey, hard place. The sky was usually the colour of wet slate, and the air smelled of exhaust and industrial decline. Police resources were stretched to the breaking point trying to keep a lid on a pressure cooker of political unrest and economic misery.

In that climate, a body found on waste ground was just another piece of bad news in a decade full of it.

Let's look at the method, because it tells us the only thing we really know about the killer. Simpson was shot. That is functional, efficient, but the fire? That is symbolic. You don't burn a body just to kill it; you burn a body to erase it. You burn it to destroy the fingerprints, the face, the clothing. You burn it to turn a human being into a question mark.

It suggests panic, or it suggests professionalism. Was it a gangland hit, incinerating any evidence? Or was it a personal rage, a desire to wipe William Simpson off the face of the earth?

We don't know where the body was found. Was it an alley in Aston? A park in Perry Barr? The records are maddeningly vague. We don't know if the fire worked, did it hide the evidence, or just flag the crime scene to the authorities?

The brutality is there, undeniable and hot. But the meaning has been stripped away. The hardest question to answer is the simplest one: Who was he?

At forty-five, Simpson had lived through the post-war reconstruction. He was old enough to remember rationing, young enough to see the city gift the world heavy metal. Did he have a wife waiting for the knock at the door? Did he have kids? Was he a factory worker, a criminal, a drifter, or a saint?

There is no public record.

This brings us to an uncomfortable truth about "True Crime." We like our victims to be photogenic. We like them to be young, preferably female, and innocent. We like a "before" photo where they are smiling at a graduation or a wedding.

William Norman Simpson was a middle-aged man in a hard city. And when middle-aged men get murdered in brutal ways, society tends to make a quiet, ugly assumption: He must have been involved in something.

We assume he took risks. We assume he owed money. We assume he was "known to the police." Whether true or not, this assumption acts like a muffler on public outcry. We don't demand justice for people we suspect might have "had it coming."

So, without a weeping widow on the news or a campaign for justice, Simpson slipped through the cracks. He became a statistic, a line item in a cold case review that

For anyone trying to research a true crime book, a case like this is a nightmare.

You cannot dramatize a void. You cannot build a narrative out of ash. There are no witnesses to interview, no suspects to speculate about.

Researching Simpson is like walking through a graveyard where the headstones have been sandblasted smooth. You know someone lies there. You know they died in pain. But you have no idea who, if anyone, mourned them. It forces you to write about the absence itself. You have to write about the silence.

In the end, William Norman Simpson is not a character in a story. He is a symptom.

He is a reminder that cities are built on top of unresolved harm. We walk over these spots every day, the street corner where a fight ended badly, the alley where a deal went wrong, the waste ground where a fire burned for an hour in May 1978.

We don't see the ghosts because we refuse to look for them.

Somewhere in the dusty archives of the West Midlands Police, there is a box. Inside that box, there might be a photo of the crime scene. There might be a report from a tired detective who clocked off his shift and went for a pint, trying to get the smell of smoke out of his nostrils.

But the box stays closed.

William Norman Simpson remains unsolved, unavenged, and largely unknown. And perhaps the most chilling thing isn't the murder itself, but the realization of how easy it is to disappear. You can be shot. You can be burned. You can die in the middle of a city of a million people.

And fifty years later, the only thing left of you is a name on a list that few ever check.

There is no twist ending here. No revelation in the final paragraph. Just a man who ceased to exist, and a city that didn't care enough to ask why.

THE FINAL REEL (OR, DEATH IN THE CINEMA)

Liverpool, 1949

On the evening of March 19, 1949, Liverpool was doing what it did best on a Saturday night: pretending the real world didn't exist.

The war had been over for four years, but nobody had told the economy. The city was still a patchwork of bomb sites and rationing books. So, people escaped. They queued in the rain to sit in the velvet dark of the picture palaces, desperate to trade their grey lives for ninety minutes of Technicolour.

At the Cameo Cinema on West Derby Road, the final show was winding down. The audience was watching the screen, lost in the flicker. But behind the auditorium, in a small, cramped office, a very different kind of drama was playing out.

Leonard Thomas, the manager, and Bernard Catterall, his deputy, were counting the day's takings. It was a mundane ritual. A bit of arithmetic, a cup of tea, and then home.

Neither of them would make it out of the building.

The robbery, if you can call it that, was a disaster from the first second. A man burst into the office. He was armed, a rarity in 1949 Britain, where villains usually favoured a razor or a length of lead pipe. Accounts differ on whether he was masked or just shadowy, but his intent was clear.

He didn't make a speech. He didn't ask for the safe combination. He just started shooting, hitting Thomas and Catterall at close range. They collapsed amidst the paperwork and the scattered cash. The gunman grabbed what he could, which turned out to be a pitiful amount, and fled into the Liverpool night.

By the time help arrived, the two men were dead.

The city reeled. A murder in a pub is one thing; a pub is a place of vice and volatility. But a cinema? A cinema is a sanctuary. It's where you take your sweetheart. It's where you take your kids. The idea that a gunman could walk into the administrative heart of the Cameo and execute two men felt an alien concept.

In 1949, the Liverpool Police were under immense pressure. The city was on edge. Trust in the authorities was fragile. They needed a result, and they needed it yesterday. When the police need a result that badly, they usually find one.

The investigation was frantic. Witnesses were questioned until their stories started to blur. Rumours flew through the docks and the tenements. And pretty soon, the police had two names: George Kelly and Charles Connolly. They were local men, known petty criminals, and each had previous for theft.

The case built against them, however, was a house of cards held together by glue and desperation. There was no forensic evidence linking them to the gun. The witness descriptions were inconsistent. But the prosecution had a narrative: two thugs, a robbery gone wrong, a cold-blooded killing.

The jury bought it. Or at least, they bought it enough. George Kelly was sentenced to death. Charles Connolly, arguably the luckier of the pair, went to prison.

On March 28, 1950, George Kelly was hanged at Walton Prison. He reportedly told the chaplain, "I am innocent. God help me." The state pulled the lever. The trapdoor opened. The case was closed.

But in true crime, "closed" is just a euphemism for "buried."

Almost immediately, the cracks began to show. The witness statements didn't line up. The timelines were impossible. A man named Donald Johnson actually confessed to the crime, but the police, having already pinned their medals on Kelly's conviction, dismissed it.

Decades passed. The world changed. But the Cameo Cinema case refused to stay dead.

Journalists and legal scholars began to pick at the scabs. They found a case that looked less like justice and more like a stitch-up. Evidence had been suppressed. Alibis had been ignored. Identifications had been coerced.

In 2003—fifty-three years too late—the Court of Appeal quashed George Kelly's conviction. He was posthumously acquitted, leaving the case officially unsolved.

This brings us to the most chilling realization of the entire saga. The Cameo Cinema murders didn't claim two victims. They claimed three.

Leonard Thomas and Bernard Catterall were murdered by a gunman.

George Kelly was murdered by the British legal system.

So, who really pulled the trigger?

That is the question that hangs over West Derby Road like a fog. If Kelly was innocent, and the courts now say he was, then a double murderer walked free in 1949. He likely lived out his life in the city, perhaps walking past the Cameo, perhaps sitting in the cinema seats, watching films in the dark, knowing what he had done.

The case exists in a strange, liminal state. Officially, there is no killer. Morally, there is no resolution.

The Cameo Cinema is gone now, the building repurposed, the screen dark. But the story remains a jagged scar on the city's history. It is a reminder that justice is not a science; it is a machine run by humans, and humans panic.

When the police are desperate and the public is frightened, the truth is often the first thing to be sacrificed. Liverpool wanted an answer. The courts gave them a name. Whether it was the right name didn't seem to matter, until the man was already in the ground, and by then it was far too late.

There is a haunting symmetry to the Cameo murders.

The audience that night left the cinema thinking the show was over. They walked out into the cool night air, complaining about the plot or praising the actors, completely unaware that the real tragedy had taken place just a few feet away, behind a closed door.

The film ended. The credits rolled.

But for the families of Thomas, Catterall, and Kelly, the lights never really came back on. And somewhere in the history of Liverpool, a gunman is still running, nameless, faceless, and unpunished, fading into the black and white grain of the past.

THE MAN ABOVE THE LAUNDRY (OR, THE STEAM THAT HID THE BLOOD)

Liverpool, 1946

In early February 1946, Liverpool was a city nursing a monumental hangover.

The war was technically over, but nobody had told the city's architecture or its stomach, rationing was still biting hard – a diet of powdered egg and grey bread. The buildings were still scarred, there were jagged gaps in the terraces where the Luftwaffe had done their worst. The docks were screaming with activity again, but the people were exhausted. It was a city moving through the motions of peace, but carrying the muscle memory of war.

And then there was Scotland Road.

"Scotty Road" wasn't just a street; it was a universe. It was the main artery of working-class Liverpool, a chaotic, cobbled canyon of tenements, pubs, and small businesses. It was a place where life was lived on the doorstep, where privacy was a luxury nobody could afford, and where everybody knew everybody else's business. Or at least, they thought they did.

At Number 44 Scotland Road, there was a small laundry. It was the kind of place you walked past without actually seeing, windows steamed up, the smell of starch and hot iron drifting out into the cold damp of the street. It was run by a man named Jaw Kay.

On a freezing night in early February, while the city shivered in its sleep, someone walked into Number 44. They climbed the stairs. And they turned a quiet bedroom into a slaughterhouse.

Jaw Kay was fifty-seven years old. In the parlance of 1946, he was simply "The Chinaman," a label that carried with it a blend of exoticism and dismissal. Liverpool has the oldest Chinese community in Europe, a legacy of the Blue Funnel Line and the tea trade, but in the mid-40s, it was still a community that often existed in parallel to the rest of the city.

Jaw Kay was a fixture. He was the man who washed the collars and pressed the sheets. He was polite, he was hard-working, and he was solitary. He lived alone in the rooms above the business, a life measured in cycles of wash, rinse, spin, repeat.

He was known, but he wasn't known. He was part of the texture of Scotland Road, like the gas lamps or the tram lines. You noticed him when you needed him, and you forgot him when you didn't.

And that invisibility would become the defining feature of his death. The timeline is blurry, lost in the fog of a pre-digital age. It was either the late hours of February 1st or the early hours of February 2nd.

The killer entered through the shop. There was no sign of a break-in, no smashed glass. What we do know is that they went upstairs to the bedroom where Jaw Kay lay sleeping.

The violence that followed was not the work of a professional thief. A thief wants to get in, get the cash, and get out. If they have to kill, it's a single blow, a means to an end.

Jaw Kay was stabbed nineteen times. Let that number sink in. Nineteen.

This wasn't a struggle. It wasn't a fight. The wounds were concentrated around his chest and throat. These were intimate, furious injuries inflicted at close range. It was an act of obliteration. The killer didn't just want him dead; they wanted him destroyed.

And yet, downstairs, the laundry was undisturbed. No overturned chairs. No scattered receipts. The violence was contained entirely within the four walls of the bedroom, a localized storm of rage while the rest of the building stood silent.

The police were initially summoned not because someone was concerned for his welfare, instead, it was a patron of the business angry that the door was locked and that they couldn't collect their washing.

The police, perhaps sensing something was off, perhaps not, forced entry into the building and found the body upstairs. The police canvassed the community. Scotland Road was a place of eyes. There are always people watching, women scrubbing steps, men smoking in doorways, kids playing in the gutters. And yet, the killer slipped through this surveillance net like a ghost.

There was a sighting, of course. There is always a sighting. A witness reported seeing a man leaving the laundry shortly after the estimated time of the attack. The description? A man in a dark coat.

In Liverpool in February 1946, everyone was a man in a dark coat. It was the uniform of the city. He wasn't running. He wasn't covered in blood (or at least, if he was the darkness of the coat hid it). He simply stepped out of the door and walked away, swallowed by the fog and the flow of the city. He walked out of history as quickly as he had walked into it.

The police reached for the standard play book: Robbery. It made sense on paper. A shopkeeper living alone? He must have a cash box. He must have the week's takings under the mattress.

But the scene didn't fit the script. There was no evidence of a frantic search. The floorboards weren't ripped up. The cupboards weren't emptied. If money was taken, it was taken quietly, and plenty was left behind. Why rob someone and then leave a significant amount of cash behind?

And then there was the brutality. You don't stab a man nineteen times for the contents of a till. You stab a man nineteen times because you hate him. Or because he betrayed you. Or, covering all options, because you are insane.

Was it a Tong war? A gambling debt? A personal vendetta? The rumours flew, fed by the stereotypes of the time. But Jaw Kay wasn't known to be a gambler or a gangster. He was a laundryman. His life appeared to be a flat line of routine.

If he had a secret life, he took it with him to the grave.

This brings us to the uncomfortable truth that hangs over this case. Why do we know about the Cameo Cinema murders, but not about Jaw Kay? Both happened in post-war Liverpool. Both were brutal. Both remain, in their own ways, unresolved.

But the Cameo murders happened in a cinema, a place of public imagination. The victims were white, British, "respectable" men doing a job that everyone understood. It was a tragedy that threatened the sanctity of the Saturday night out.

Jaw Kay was a solitary immigrant living above a shop. He had no weeping widow to give interviews to the Liverpool Echo. He had no powerful family demanding justice from the Home Secretary.

He was easy to forget.

The Cameo case became famous because the system overreacted, hanging an innocent man in a desperate bid to show control, whereas the Jaw Kay case became obscure because the system under-reacted. The police did their job, certainly. They took statements. They knocked on doors. But when the leads dried up, there was no political pressure to keep digging. The file was closed, tied with a piece of string, and placed on a shelf.

One case is a tragedy of action; the other is a tragedy of inertia.

If you go to Scotland Road today, looking for the ghost of Jaw Kay, you won't find him.

You won't even find Number 44.

The Scotland Road of 1946 is largely gone, victim to the wrecking ball of 1960s progress. The Kingsway Tunnel, the road widening schemes, the demolition of the tenements, they wiped the map clean. The bricks and mortar of the laundry have been pulverized into dust and buried under tarmac.

The physical space where Jaw Kay died no longer exists.

But history doesn't require a blue plaque to be real. It only requires that something happened, and that it was never resolved.

There is a temptation for a writer to try and fill the gaps. To invent a smoky backroom gambling den, or a lover's quarrel, or a racist attack. We want the narrative to have a shape.

But true crime isn't about fiction. It's about reality, no matter how forgotten, or frustrating.

The horror of Jaw Kay's death isn't just the nineteen stab wounds. It is the silence that follows. It is the fact that a man can be butchered in his own bed, on one of the busiest streets in the Empire, and the city simply absorbs it and moves on.

It represents a category of crime that rarely makes the Netflix documentary list:

* The private victim.

* The domestic setting.

* The total lack of resolution.

Statistically, this is what murder usually looks like. It isn't a master criminal playing chess with a detective. It is a sudden, ugly explosion of violence, followed by a long, slow fade to black.

Someone walked into that laundry. They carried a knife. They carried a grudge. And today, eighty years later, they are likely dead, having lived a whole life with the memory of what the knife felt like when it hit bone.

Jaw Kay lies in a Liverpool cemetery, far from the land of his ancestors. The laundry is gone. The steam has dissipated.

If the Cameo Cinema murders teach us what happens when justice moves too fast, the murder of Jaw Kay teaches us the opposite lesson:

It teaches us what happens when the world simply shrugs.

THE RED SHOE (OR, THE CINDERELLA OF TANG HALL)

York, 1946

In September 1946, York was a city trying to remember how to be gentle.

The war had ended the previous year, but the psychological blackout curtains were still drawn tight. Ration books were still folded in kitchen drawers next to the cutlery. The streets still bore the scars of the conflict, patches of waste ground, hastily repaired brickwork, and the lingering, bone-deep exhaustion of a population that had spent six years holding its breath.

People were slowly learning to let go. Mothers were learning to let their children wander out of eyesight again. They were relearning trust.

That trust lasted for exactly one summer.

On the evening of September 21, 1946, a four-year-old girl named Norma Mary Dale went out to play and failed to come home. By the time the sun rose the next morning, the ancient city of York had changed. The cathedral bells might have rung the same note, but the city beneath them had turned cold, suspicious, and terrified.

Norma lived in Tang Hall. To the tourists who come for the Minster and the Shambles, Tang Hall is a world away. It's a working-class district on the eastern edge of the city, a place of red brick and honest labour.

In 1946, it was a community where doors were left unlocked and neighbours knew each other by the sound of their footsteps. It was the kind of place where a child's world extended as far as their legs could carry them before tea time.

Norma was small, lively, and undeniably visible. On that Saturday, she was dressed in an outfit that her mother would later describe to the police with a heart-shattering attention to detail. But it was her feet that mattered.

She was wearing a pair of bright red leather shoes. In the grey, monochromatic world of post-war austerity, those shoes were a splash of colour. They were vibrant. They were innocent. And they would become the most haunting object in the criminal history of York.

When dusk fell and Norma didn't return, the alarm wasn't raised by a siren, but by a ripple of panic spreading door to door.

York responded as cities often do when a child vanishes: with frantic, collective, action. The police were called, but the search was driven by the community. Men finished their shifts and walked straight out into the dark. Women stood on doorsteps, calling her name.

Hundreds of torches flickered across the hedgerows and the waste grounds—those bomb-damaged plots that sat like cavities in the city's smile.

They searched with a desperation born of hope, but with a dread born of reality, everyone wanted to find her. But, as the hours ticked by, no one wanted to be the one to find her.

And yet, someone had to.

Norma's body was discovered on a patch of waste ground near Rawdon Avenue, just a few hundred yards from her home. The scene was stark and devastatingly simple. She had been strangled. There was no elaborate attempt to hide the body, no shallow grave. She was just discarded.

But it was the detail of her feet that stopped the hearts of the search party. One of her red shoes was missing. The other lay nearby, a tiny, crimson marker in the wilted grass.

Almost immediately, the press seized on it. The case became "The Red Shoe Murder." It is a grotesque name, the kind of title you'd find in a cheap paperback mystery, but it stuck because human beings need symbols. The more lurid tabloids, never known for their subtlety, dubbed her "The Cinderella of Tang Hall."

Whilst it's easy to get angry at the sensationalism, it can be a perverse form of coping. For many it's almost impossible to process the murder of a four-year-old girl; the horror is too vast, too shocking. So we focus on the object. We focus on the shoe. We make it a sound bite to distance ourselves from the horror.

The red shoe became a symbol of interrupted innocence. It was reproduced in newspapers, described on the radio. It became the key to the entire mystery. Find the other shoe, the logic went, and you find the monster.

But that shoe was gone.

This wasn't a crime committed by a stranger passing through on a train. Norma hadn't been taken to a secondary location miles away. She hadn't been bundled into a car.

She was killed on waste ground in her own neighbourhood. This proximity is what makes her murder so shocking. The killer had to have walked the same streets. He knew the waste ground. He knew the shortcuts. He likely knew the rhythm of the police patrols.

In a cathedral city steeped in history, a child murder feels like a violation of the sanctuary. Parents locked their doors. The "free range" childhood of the 1940s ended overnight in Tang Hall. Every man walking alone was a suspect. Every neighbour was re-examined.

Did he act strange yesterday? Why was he washing his clothes so late? Where was he when the search party went out?

Paranoia is a heavy mist, and it settled over York and refused to lift. The effects of poor Norma's murder were felt for generations.

The investigation was massive, but it was blind. We have to remember the era. In 1946, forensic science was practically medieval compared to today.

There was no DNA profiling to swipe from the girl's clothing. There was no CCTV to catch a shadowy figure walking away. There were no databases of offenders to cross-reference.

The police had to rely on memory. And memory, as any detective will tell you, is the most treacherous evidence of all. Witnesses came forward, but their stories blurred. Time is elastic when people are scared. Sightings overlapped and contradicted each other. A man seen here, a man seen there. A vague description of a figure in the twilight.

The police reconstructed Norma's final movements.

They tracked the red shoes as far as they could. But the trail went cold at the edge of the waste ground.

The killer didn't step forward. He didn't brag in a pub. He didn't leave a calling card. He simply committed an atrocity and then dissolved back into the population.

Weeks turned into months, then months into years, and the red shoe never reappeared.

No arrests were made. No charges were brought. The headlines moved on to the rebuilding of Europe and the Nuremberg Trials. The murder of one small girl in York couldn't compete with the weight of global history.

But for the family, and in many ways York itself, time didn't heal; it just calcified the pain.

The case file gathered dust. The killer aged. He likely walked past the crime scene a thousand times. He might have stood in the queue at the butchers next to Norma's mother. He might have died in his bed, an old man mourned by a family who never knew what his hands had done.

In 2016, exactly seventy years after the murder, North Yorkshire Police announced a review.

Advances in forensics meant that evidence preserved from 1946 might finally yield answers. It was a moment of hope. Relatives spoke to the press. Historians dusted off the archives. The red shoe, or the memory of it, was vivid again.

But reality is rarely as satisfying as fiction.

The review concluded without a definitive breakthrough. Time is a thief; it steals evidence as surely as it steals lives. DNA degrades. Witnesses die. Memories fade into nothing.

The red shoe remained missing.

There is a particular difficulty in writing about the murder of a child. The instinct is to look away, or to demand a resolution that balances the scales.

Norma Dale did not choose to be a symbol. She was just a little girl who wanted to play out. She became a legend because the system failed her, and because her death happened at a moment when Britain desperately wanted to believe the horror was over.

It wasn't.

Today, Tang Hall has changed. The houses have been modernized. The waste ground has been built over or landscaped. Children play there again, their laughter echoing over the spot where a search party once shone their torches into the face of a nightmare.

There is no blue plaque. There is no memorial garden. History rarely announces itself in the suburbs.

But somewhere in York, the truth exists. Or at least, it existed once.

Norma Mary Dale's murder represents the quietest, saddest category of British crime: the local tragedy that never ends. It is a story about a shoe that was lost, and a peace that was broken.

The red shoe, bright and unmistakable, was the only thing left behind. Everything else, the killer, the motive, the truth, vanished into the Yorkshire night.

And in that absence, the city learned a difficult lesson: that sometimes, the monster isn't under the bed. Sometimes, he is just the man walking quietly down the street, and he takes his secrets to the grave.

THE SILENCE OF MOSS SIDE (OR, THE MAN WHO TALKED TOO MUCH)

Manchester, 1965

In the 1960s, Manchester was swinging. It was a city of beat clubs, sharp suits, and northern soul. It was the era of George Best weaving magic at Old Trafford and the twisting, turning optimism of a post-war generation finding its voice.

But beneath the pop songs and the bright lights, there was another Manchester. This was a city of hard men, protection rackets, and unlicensed drinking dens known as "shebeens." It was a city where the police and the villains often drank in the same pubs, maintaining an uneasy truce that occasionally exploded into violence.

In the mid-60s, the centre of gravity for this shadow world was Moss Side. Before the riots of the 80s and the "Gunchester" headlines of the 90s, Moss Side was a tight grid of Victorian terraces, struggling with poverty and teeming with life. It was here, in the cold January of 1965, that a small-time criminal named James "Little Jimmy" Evans met an end so brutal it silenced an entire neighbourhood.

Jimmy wasn't a kingpin. He wasn't a mastermind. He was a grifter, a chancer, a man operating on the fringes of the legendary Quality Street Gang.

But Jimmy had a problem. He didn't know when to keep his mouth shut. And in the underworld of 1960s Manchester, silence wasn't just golden; it was the only life insurance policy that paid out.

Jimmy Evans was thirty-two years old. He was a flash character, the kind of man who liked to be seen. He wore mohair suits, drove a Ford Zodiac, and always had a roll of banknotes in his pocket—even if he'd had to borrow them an hour earlier.

He ran a club. Well, "club" is a generous term. It was an illegal gambling joint and drinking den in a terraced house on the borders of Moss Side and Whalley Range. It was the kind of place where the curtains stayed closed at noon and the air was thick with the smell of stale beer and Capstan Full Strength.

Jimmy was ambitious. He wanted to be a player. But ambition in the underworld is dangerous if you don't have the muscle to back it up.

Jimmy had stepped on toes. He had reportedly been talking to the police, or at least, bragging that he could talk to the police if he wanted to. He had also been skimming off the top of some he worked for, all whilst undercutting the wrong people in the protection game, making himself a list of enemies.

There were even rumours that he had fallen foul of the "K" family, a notorious Manchester crime dynasty (though never proven). Others said he had upset the Quality Street Gang, the shadowy syndicate that supposedly ran the city's security rackets.

Whoever he upset, they didn't send him a warning. They sent him an execution squad.

On the night of January 18, 1965, Jimmy was at a house

in Bruton Street, Moss Side. It wasn't his house. It was a safe house, or perhaps a trap house. He was there with his young son, barely a toddler, who was sleeping in the next room.

Around midnight, there was a knock at the door, and Jimmy answered it. He likely knew the men standing on the step. In that world, you are rarely killed by a stranger. You are killed by someone you drank with the night before.

They didn't just shoot him, though, that would have been too quick. That would have been business. This was personal.

What happened over the next hour was a lesson in sadism. The details are grim. Jimmy was beaten with iron bars. He was kicked. He was slashed. The autopsy would later reveal dozens upon dozens of injuries. It was a prolonged, methodical, torture of a human being.

Crucially, the beating was concentrated on his head and his mouth. It was a message written in bone and blood: This is what happens to a man who talks.

Finally, as he lay broken on the floor, one of the men produced a shotgun and shot him, in what was left of his face, at point blank range.

And then, with the smell of cordite hanging in the damp air, they walked out into the Manchester night, leaving a toddler sleeping upstairs and a dead man cooling on the linoleum.

The murder of Little Jimmy Evans was a sensation. It was gangland violence spilling out onto the front pages. The Manchester City Police (this was before the formation of the GMP) launched a massive investigation. They pulled in every known face in the city. They kicked down doors in Moss Side, Cheetham

Hill, and Salford.

Detectives knew who did it. Or at least, they were confident that they knew who ordered it. But knowing something and proving are two different things

The names of the hitmen were whispered in every pub from the Spread Eagle to the Ritz. They were allegedly "The scouse lads," hired muscle brought in from Liverpool to keep the Manchester hands clean. Though the rumours in other parts of the city was that they were local hard men, rising stars making their bones.

The police investigation hit a brick wall. It was a wall built of fear. Witnesses developed sudden amnesia. Men who had seen the killers' car suddenly couldn't remember the colour. People who had been in the house minutes before the attack claimed they were on the other side of town. One officer quipped, dryly, that he was surprised witnesses could even remember their own names.

Even Jimmy's associates, the people who supposedly drank with him? shrugged their shoulders. Jimmy? Nice lad. Flash. Shame about the face. No idea who did it, officer.

The Omertà of Manchester was absolute.

Detective Superintendent Arthur Benfield led the hunt. He was an old-school copper, a man who wore a trilby and a raincoat and believed in the rules. He was furious as he knew he was being played.

In a move that smacked of desperation, the police took the unusual step of issuing "threat to life" warnings to other criminals. They believed a war was coming. They believed Jimmy's friends would retaliate.

But there was no war. There was no retaliation.

Why? Because Jimmy didn't have friends. He had acquaintances, plenty of those, and he had customers. But friend? They were in short supply. In the cold calculus of the underworld, he was a liability. His death was accepted as a necessary housekeeping measure. The balance of power had been restored.

The investigation dragged on for months. Several men were arrested. One was even charged, a well-known local villain, but the case against him was circumstantial. The Director of Public Prosecutions dropped the charges before it even reached trial meaning that the police had to release him. He walked out of the station with a smirk, knowing that the silence had held.

The death of Jimmy Evans is often cited as the moment the "Quality Street Gang" came of age.

Whether the gang existed as a formal organization or was just a loose collective of friends is a matter of debate (and legal action) to this day. But the myth of them became powerful.

They were the men who supposedly ran Manchester. They were the men who (allegedly) inspired the Thin Lizzy song The Boys Are Back in Town. They were charming, violent, and untouchable. The press coined their nickname, as when encountered they resembled a group of characters from a popular 1960s advert for tins of Quality Street chocolate. The Manchester of the 1990s saw Gangstas clad in tracksuits. The Quality Street gang would not have approved – their style was as important to them as their grip on the city.

Jimmy's murder sent a signal to everyone in the city: We can get to anyone. We can do it in your own home. And we can do it with the police watching. It changed the atmosphere of the city. Amateur hour was over and the era of the "hard man" had arrived.

Sixty years later, Bruton Street has changed. The slums were cleared in the huge redevelopment projects of the late 60s and 70s. The geography of Moss Side was rewritten with concrete and flyovers.

The house where Jimmy died is gone, buried under the foundations of a new estate or a community centre. But the murder of Little Jimmy Evans remains one of Manchester's darkest open secrets.

Jimmy Evans wanted to be famous. He wanted to be a name on everyone's lips. He got his wish but paid the ultimate price.

He died because he broke the golden rule of the north: See all, hear all, say nowt.

And because he couldn't keep quiet, the city kept quiet for him.

The killers of Little Jimmy Evans got away with it. They likely grew old. Some of them supposedly became legitimate businessmen. Some of them died in their beds, respected grandfathers who never told their families about the night they walked into a house in Moss Side and blew a man away.

The police file is still open, gathering dust in a basement somewhere in Greater Manchester. But it will never be solved. The witnesses are dead. The evidence is gone.

All that remains is the story. A warning from the ghosts of the 60s:

In Manchester, you can be loud, you can be flash, and you can be dangerous. But you must never, ever, be a grass.

THE STATIONMASTER'S LAST SHIFT (OR, A TICKET TO NOWHERE)

Gateshead, 1911

Lintz Green was never meant to be a place where history happened.

It sat quietly on the railway line between Newcastle and Consett, a small rural punctuation mark in a sentence written by the North Eastern Railway. It served scattered farms, the odd pit village, and the dense, brooding woodlands that blurred the boundary between Gateshead and County Durham.

Trains stopped there because the timetable said they must, not because the world demanded it. It was a place of steam, silence, and routine.

On the evening of October 7, 1911, that routine was shattered by a single gunshot.

By the time the sun rose the next morning, Lintz Green Station had been transformed from a sleepy halt into a crime scene, entering the long, uncomfortable history of Britain's unresolved mysteries.

In 1911, Britain was running on railway time. The network stitched the country together, shrinking distances and redefining the workday. But while the cities roared with progress, stations like Lintz Green remained resolutely small. They were places where the staff knew the passengers by the cut of their coats, and where a stranger on the platform was an event in itself.

George Wilson was the stationmaster. He was part of the furniture.

He lived nearby, walking the short, familiar distance between the station and his home at the end of every shift. He was sixty years old. He was trusted, respected, and thoroughly unremarkable. He was the sort of man whose name appears in the local paper only twice: once when he marries, and once when he dies.

That night, Wilson was closing up. The last train had wheezed its way through to Blackhill. The platform was empty, lit only by the weak, flickering gas lamps that cast long, dancing shadows across the gravel. The silence of the Derwent Valley was settling in.

Wilson followed his ritual. He locked the booking office. He checked the signals. He extinguished the lights.

He stepped onto the path leading home, a path he had walked a thousand times.

Only this time, he didn't make it.

The violence was sudden and absolute.

Just moments after stepping into the darkness of the station approach, Wilson was shot. The bullet struck him at close range. He collapsed near the station grounds, fatally wounded, bleeding out into the dirt of the path he kept so tidy.

There was no sign of a prolonged struggle. No drawn-out confrontation. Whoever pulled the trigger knew exactly what they were doing, or, at the very least, knew that speed was the difference between a murder and a hanging.

Wilson managed to crawl a short distance, but by the

time help arrived, alerted by the crack of the gunshot echoing through the trees, the stationmaster was already dead.

The murder of a railway stationmaster was rare. The murder of one in such a quiet, isolated location was almost unheard of.

From the moment the police arrived, they were chasing shadows. This wasn't a city crime. There were no crowded tenements to canvas, no gin palaces to dredge for witnesses. But it wasn't a simple rural crime either.

The railway connected Lintz Green to the world. The killer could have come from Newcastle, Gateshead, or Consett. They could have jumped a freight train. They could have vanished into the dense woods that lined the tracks.

And then there was the weapon. In Edwardian Britain, you didn't just stumble across a firearm. This was before the flood of service revolvers that would return from the Great War three years later. Guns were rare, particularly in rural Durham.

The presence of a gun raised immediate, uncomfortable questions. Was this a professional hit? Was it a poacher gone rogue? Was it a stolen weapon? In a world before widespread gun registration, the pistol was a ghost. It was never found, and without it, the police were trying to solve a puzzle with the most important piece missing.

The detectives did what detectives do: they looked for the money. Railway stations handled cash. Ticket sales, freight charges, it all added up. Perhaps Wilson had been targeted for the day's takings.

But the theory fell apart almost immediately. There was no evidence of theft. Wilson's pockets hadn't been rifled. The station safe wasn't blown. If this was a robbery, it was the most incompetent one in the history of the North East, or the most easily distracted.

Then came the theory of mistaken identity. Had the killer been waiting for someone else? A rival? A debtor? Had poor George Wilson just walked into a bullet meant for another man?

It's a comforting thought—that the tragedy was an accident of timing. But no alternative target ever emerged. No one else on the line reported a feud. And the killer had been close enough to see Wilson's face, or at least his uniform.

The investigation was hampered by the geography. Lintz Green sat in an awkward administrative limbo.

It was close enough to Gateshead to feel like part of its orbit, yet technically aligned with County Durham. This mattered more than it should have. Jurisdictional boundaries are the enemy of good policing. Information moved slowly between forces. Coordination was imperfect.

The railway connected places seamlessly. The police forces at the time did not. As the weeks dragged on, the pressure mounted. The public was scared. The North Eastern Railway was embarrassed. They needed a suspect.

And eventually, they found one.

Samuel Atkinson was a railway porter. He worked on the line. He was known to the station. He fit the profile of a local man with access and opportunity. He was arrested and charged with the wilful murder of George Wilson.

The newspapers breathed a sigh of relief. The railway

authorities nodded sagely. A trial would provide answers and a hanging would provide closure.

But when the case reached the magistrates' court, something extraordinary happened. The prosecution stood up and, essentially, shrugged and offered no evidence.

The case against Atkinson was circumstantial at best, non-existent at worst. There was no weapon. There was no witness. There was no motive that stuck. The magistrates had no choice but to dismiss the charges.

Atkinson walked free, and with that, the investigation effectively died.

The decision not to proceed remains one of the most baffling aspects of the Lintz Green case. Why charge a man only to abandon the case entirely before a jury could even look at it? Was the evidence flawed? Had a witness recanted? Or had the police simply grabbed the most convenient suspect to appease the press, only to realise they had nothing to back it up?

Official records offer no clear explanation. Just a sudden, grinding halt.

George Wilson became another name in a dusty ledger.

But the station didn't forget. Trains continued to stop at Lintz Green. Passengers waited on the same platform where the killer had lurked. Staff worked the same hours, lighting the same lamps that Wilson had extinguished for the last time.

But the atmosphere had changed.

Those who worked the line remembered. They walked the platform differently. They listened more carefully to footsteps on the gravel after dark. They looked twice at figures standing alone in the shadows of the booking hall. As with many such cases, a place's innocence was lost, leaving the station carrying a memory it could not shake. It became a place defined by what had happened there, a landmark of violence in a landscape of trees and tracks.

For the true-crime writer, the Lintz Green Station murder is a study in frustration.

There is no twist. There is no confession. There is no late-breaking forensic revelation from a cold case unit (the station and the evidence are long gone). There is only a brief, brutal moment of violence, followed by administrative failure and then a systemic forgetting.

It is not a case that demands attention; it waits quietly for it.

No one saw the shot fired. No one saw the killer leave.

The railway line, designed to connect people, became the perfect escape route. The killer could have been in Newcastle drinking a pint within an hour, or deep in the Durham dales.

1911 was a year of tension in Britain. Industrial unrest was simmering. Strikes were looming. The railways were central to all of it, symbols of progress, control, and vulnerability. Was Wilson's murder connected to that wider unrest? A grudge against the company taken out on its representative?

There is no evidence for it. But violence rarely occurs in a vacuum.

Lintz Green Station is long closed. It was shut down in the 1950s, a victim of the Beeching cuts and the rise of the motorcar.

Nature has reclaimed much of the surrounding land. The trackbed is now the Derwent Walk, a footpath for hikers and cyclists. The rhythms of 1911 are gone. The steam has evaporated.

There is no plaque. No marker. No sign to indicate that a murder occurred here. History does not announce itself at Lintz Green.

But if you walk that path on an October evening, when the light is fading and the trees cast long shadows across the trail, it is easy to imagine the smell of coal smoke and the rattle of a distant train.

George Wilson's final journey was a short one, from the station door to the path home. He never arrived.

And somewhere between Gateshead and Durham, between railway time and human time, a single unanswered gunshot still echoes, not loudly, but persistently, in the strange, unsettled margins of Britain's past.

The killer walked away into the dark. And over a century later, we are still staring into the trees, wondering who was looking back.

THE VASE ON THE MANTELPIECE (OR, THE QUIET DEATH OF A QUIET MAN)

Leicester, 1965

In 1965, Leicester was a city that measured its pulse in the ticking of factory clocks and the whir of knitting machines.

It was the hosiery capital of Europe, a place of steady work, red brick terraces, and a sense of civic solidity. It wasn't swinging London. It wasn't the rough-and-tumble docks of Liverpool. It was the Midlands. Sensible, central, and safe. The war was twenty years in the rear-view mirror, and the bomb sites had largely been paved over. Violence, the locals believed, was something that happened elsewhere.

That belief died on the same day as Sidney Leeson.

Sidney was seventy-five years old. He lived alone. He was retired. He was one of thousands of men in post-war Britain who occupied the quiet margins of society, visible enough to be nodded at, but invisible enough to be ignored.

And then, he was beaten to death in his own front room.

Sidney Leeson wasn't rich. He wasn't famous. He didn't have a scandalous past or a secret fortune buried under the floorboards. His life, by all accounts, was a masterpiece of the unremarkable. This is not an insult; it's a tragedy. Because when a man lives that quietly, his death often follows suit.

He lived in a house that was likely tidy, smelling of old tea and coal dust. He had his routines. He had his pension. And on a day that began like any other, he had a visitor.

The police found him dead on the floor. The cause of death was blunt force trauma. He hadn't been shot by a gangster or poisoned by a femme fatale. He had been bludgeoned.

The murder weapon? A vase. It had been taken from inside the house. It was a crime of horrifying domestic intimacy. One minute, the vase was sitting on a shelf or a mantelpiece, a mundane object of decoration. The next, it was being used to crush a man's skull.

The most chilling detail of the Leeson case is what wasn't there. There was no smashed window. There was no splintered door frame. In 1965, Britain was a different country. It was the era of the latchkey, of back doors left on the hook, of trusting a stranger because they wore a tie or a uniform. Safeguarding wasn't a concept yet, community care for the elderly was at best informal, if it existed at all. And if someone knocked at the door, you opened it.

Sidney Leeson almost certainly let his killer in. Did he know them? Was it a neighbour? A distant relative? Or was it simply a chancer, someone selling dusters or asking for a glass of water, who saw a frail old man as an opportunity?

The lack of forced entry turns the crime from a break-in into a betrayal. It suggests a moment of conversation, perhaps even a cup of tea, before the atmosphere curdled and the violence began.

Money was taken. The police seized on this immediately. Motive: Robbery. Case closed? Not quite. Robbery explains the entry, but it doesn't explain the butchery. If you are young enough and strong enough to rob a seventy-five-year-old man, you don't need to kill him. You certainly don't need to beat him repeatedly with a piece of ceramics until he stops moving.

This wasn't a snatch-and-grab. This was rage. Or panic. Or perhaps it showed a cold, sadistic willingness to eliminate the only witness to a petty theft. The killer traded a human life for a handful of cash. It is a brutal arithmetic that left detectives staring at the wall, trying to understand the kind of mind that makes that calculation.

The investigation began with the usual flurry of activity. Officers in heavy wool coats knocked on doors. They walked the grid of streets. They asked the neighbours: Did you see anyone? Did you hear anything? But they were met with silence.

Leicester was changing. New communities were arriving; old neighbourhoods were being redeveloped. The tight-knit fabric of the street was fraying just enough for a killer to slip through.

When it came to physical evidence the crime scene offered nothing. The vase was a dead end. In 1965, you couldn't swab the handle for touch DNA. Fingerprints were only useful if the killer had a record and had been careless enough to leave a perfect impression on a curved surface.

There were no witnesses. No one saw a man running

down the street clutching a wad of notes. No one saw a bloodstained coat. The killer simply stepped out of Sidney's front door, closed it behind him, and vanished into the city.

One of the hardest truths in true crime is that publicity matters. If Sidney Leeson had been a young woman, or a wealthy socialite, the press would have camped on his lawn. They would have given the killer a nickname: The Vase Murderer or The Twilight Years Killer.

But Sidney was an old man. And sadly, society often has a high tolerance for the suffering of the elderly. There was no campaign. There were no front-page splashes demanding justice. The case was reported as a sad fact, not a sensational story. It lacked the "hook" that keeps a cold case alive in the public imagination.

Momentum is oxygen to an investigation. Without it, the fire goes out. The detectives moved on to fresher crimes. The file on Sidney Leeson grew thinner, then dusty, then forgotten.

Sidney Leeson's house is still there, or at least the plot of land is. The bricks might have changed, but the space remains. Someone else lives there now. They watch TV in the room where he died. They put flowers in a vase on the mantelpiece, unaware of the echo in the walls.

The murder of Sidney Leeson represents a category of crime that, as we've already seen, is statistically common but narratively invisible. It is the "Quiet Murder."

They are the murder cases that slip through the cracks because they are too ordinary to be remembered. They don't have the glamour of a gangland hit or the mystery of a locked-room puzzle. They are just a nasty, brutish act, committed for a few pounds.

In the archives of the Leicestershire Police, there is likely an index card. It reads:

1965. Leeson, Sidney. Beaten to Death. Unsolved.

That line contains the entire tragedy. It acknowledges the death, but it offers no resolution.

To date there have been no deathbed confessions. No cold case breakthroughs with new technology as there was likely no evidence preserved to test. The killer got away with it. They lived their life, spent the money, and grew old—a privilege they denied to Sidney.

Sidney Leeson lived a life that passed largely unnoticed, and he died a death that followed the same pattern. This is what makes this case particularly unsettling. Not the gore, or the mystery, but the banality of evil.

It reminds us that you don't need to be special to be a target. You don't need enemies. You just need to be old, alone, and behind a door that opens too easily.

A vase shattered. A man died. And a city moved on.

THE GIRL IN THE TREE (OR, HOW TO HIDE A BODY IN THE WEST MIDLANDS)

Worcestershire, 1943

If you were to design the perfect setting for a Gothic murder mystery, you would probably come up with Hagley Wood. It sits on the edge of the Clent Hills in Worcestershire, a place that manages to look moody and atmospheric even when the sun is trying its best. It is a landscape of ancient trees, rolling fogs, and the sort of silence that feels like the entire world is holding its breath.

In 1943, however, the local residents weren't thinking about Gothic literature. They were thinking about the Luftwaffe, rationing, and how to acquire a rabbit or two for the stew pot without the local gamekeeper noticing.

This brings us to April 18, 1943, and four teenage boys: Bob Farmer, Robert Hart, Thomas Willetts, and Fred Payne. They were in Hagley Wood for the express purpose of "bird-nesting," which is the polite historical euphemism for poaching. They were looking for eggs, birds, or anything edible that wasn't powdered.

As they crept through the undergrowth, attempting to be invisible, they stumbled upon a wych elm. It was a gnarled, dying thing, looking less like a tree and more like an angry arthritic hand clawing its way out of the earth. It was also hollow—a perfect spot for a bird's nest.

Bob Farmer, the boldest of the quartet, volunteered to scale it. He scrambled up the trunk and peered into the hollow cavity, hoping for an owl or a wood pigeon. Instead, he found himself staring into the empty eye sockets of a human skull.

After much deliberation the boys decided to put it back, as they were worried about getting told off for trespassing, and the more serious crime of poaching.

It's a uniquely British reaction to a murder: 'Yes, it's a dead body, but we really shouldn't be on Lord Cobham's grass.'

"It's probably just an animal," another of them likely lied, despite the fact that few badgers have human teeth and hair, fearing the trouble they'd be in for poaching.

They agreed to a solemn pact of silence. They would never speak of this. They would take the secret to their graves. A pact lasted roughly four hours. By the time he got home, the youngest of the group, Thomas Willetts, was feeling the crushing weight of having seen a dead person. He cracked, told his father, and the police were summoned.

When the Worcestershire police arrived, they found that Bob hadn't been hallucinating. Inside the trunk was a near-complete female skeleton. She had been placed there whole, presumably while the body was still warm and pliable, because apparently fitting a fully rigid human into a tree trunk is a logistical nightmare.

Professor James Webster, a forensic pathologist, conducted the examination. He concluded the woman had been dead for about 18 months, placing her death around October 1941. She was roughly 35 years old, five feet tall, and had mousey brown hair.

But it was the details that made the case unsettling. First, there was the shoe. A single crepe-soled shoe was found near the body. Just one. Where was the other? Did she hop into the woods? Did the killer keep it as a souvenir?

Second, and far more grim, was the mouth. Inside the skull's jaw, Webster found a wad of taffeta. It wasn't just placed there; it had been forced down her throat. She hadn't died from the exposure or the tree-stuffing; she had been asphyxiated.

The police had a body, a murder weapon (the taffeta), and a location. What they didn't have was a name. They checked missing persons records. They cross-referenced dental charts, as she had very irregular distinctive teeth, and contacted dentists across the country.

Nothing.

It seemed the woman had simply popped into existence inside the tree, specifically to confuse the local constabulary. The war didn't help, of course. In 1941 and 1942, people moved around constantly. Women took factory jobs in new cities; men went overseas; houses were bombed. If someone went missing, it was easy to assume they'd just "gone to help the war effort" or been lost in a raid.

The case began to go cold. The files began gathering dust. The police were baffled. And then, just as the case seemed destined to slip from memory, the graffiti started.

Around Christmas of 1943, some six months after the discovery, a message appeared in white chalk on a wall in Upper Dean Street, Birmingham. It read:

WHO PUT LUEBELLA DOWN THE WYCH ELM?

It was specific. It was odd. And it suggested that someone knew something.

Initially, the police assumed it was a prank. But then another appeared. And another. The spelling varied, the phrasing shifted slightly, but the core message was always the same. Finally, after around two dozen variations, the copy editors of the vandal world settled on the standardised version that would become legendary:

WHO PUT BELLA IN THE WYCH ELM?

Suddenly, the victim had a name. Bella. Was it her real name? Was it a nickname? Or was the graffiti artist just inspired by the news story? No one knew but the name stuck.

The graffiti appeared on the base of the Hagley Obelisk. It appeared on walls in and around Birmingham. It was relentless. Every time the authorities scrubbed it off, it reappeared, again and again. It turned a grim murder case into a local piece of folklore. It was no longer just a forensic puzzle; it was a taunt. It had become legend.

So, who was Bella? Over the decades, two main theories have risen to the top, and both are wild enough to be the plot of a Sunday night ITV drama.

Theory One: The German Cabaret Singer

This theory is the favourite of anyone who likes their murder mysteries to include war time espionage and parachuting German spies.

In 1953, a cousin of the original pathologist contacted the police. He claimed that documents found in a German spy archive suggested that "Bella" was actually Clara Bauerle.

Clara was a cabaret singer and actress who had been the lover of a German agent named Josef Jakobs. Jakobs has the dubious distinction of being the last man executed at the Tower of London, having been caught parachuting into Cambridgeshire in 1941. He'd been caught arguably the most stereotypically German items imaginable in his possession: a Nazi secret radio and a large German sausage.

The theory goes that Clara was supposed to parachute in with him, or shortly after. However, she landed in the West Midlands, got into trouble, and was silenced by a fellow spy in order to protect the mission.

It fits the timeline. Clara Bauerle disappeared from the German stage and screen in 1941. Her height matched the skeleton. She had teeth that, from photographs at least, matched the skeleton. And, most tellingly, she was never seen again.

If this theory is true, it paints a tragic picture. A woman parachutes into a hostile country, perhaps realising too late that espionage involves less glamour than portrayed in fiction, and far more hiding in wet woods, only to be murdered by her own side and unceremoniously posed into a tree. It's an end unbefitting for a cabaret star.

It's also curious to point out that few writers have ever explored the idea that she may have landed nearby, was killed by a local as a spy, who then stashed her in the tree before making off with her parachute. Silk was in high demand and short supply. A parachute could be put to much better use for the women of the West Midlands.

Theory Two: The Witchcraft Ritual

Because this was rural England, we cannot escape the "Witchcraft" theory. This was championed by the anthropologist Margaret Murray, who suggested the murder was an occult execution.

Murray pointed out that the hand of the skeleton had been severed and buried separately near the tree, though it's worth pointing out that police believed that this most likely would have been caused by animals, moving the bones postmortem. But the police's theory didn't stop Murray who argued that the removal of the hand was consistent with the "Hand of Glory," a ritualistic object used by burglars and witches to... well, the specifics are vary depending on the belief in the part of the country you're in, but it's generally considered a black magic object to be used for nefarious purposes.

She also noted that "Wych Elm" sounds a bit like "Witch Elm." While this theory was fantastic for selling newspapers, it falls apart under scrutiny. Occultists are generally quite organized; and stuffing a body into a tree feels less like a ritual and more like a panic. Furthermore, during the height of WWII, most people were too busy worrying about Hitler to organize elaborate woodland sacrifices.

Theory Three: The Dutch Connection

In 1953, the police received a letter from a woman calling herself "Anna." She claimed that in 1942, her husband, a Dutchman working for a spy ring, had confessed to the murder.

According to Anna, her husband and a Dutch

collaborator had been driving with a Dutch woman, presumably Bella, who was threatening to expose their operation. In a panic, they strangled her in the car. Terrified of being caught with a body, they drove to the woods and—in a moment of desperate improvisation—hid her in the tree.

This theory has the ring of truth to it. It explains the lack of preparation (the taffeta gag was likely something at hand, perhaps originally a scarf). It explains the haphazard disposal. It explains why no local woman was ever reported missing.

But Anna, true to the mysterious nature of the case, disappeared into the ether. Her husband had died years prior.

Today, the most frustrating part of the Bella mystery isn't the lack of suspects, it's the lack of Bella herself.

Sometime in the early 1970s, the police wished to re-examine the remains using modern technology. They went to the Birmingham University Medical School, where the bones were stored, only they were gone.

The skull, the skeleton, the shoe, all of it had vanished. Nobody knows if they had been thrown out accidentally during a clear-out, if they were stolen by a macabre collector, or were simply misplaced by a disorganized professor.

So, today, we're left with a murder with no body. We have a crime scene that was just a tree, and which has since died and been removed, and we have a name that is likely to be fake.

And yet, the graffiti remains. Every few years, someone repaints the message on the Wychbury Obelisk. It has become a rite of passage, a local tradition.

ADRIAN FINNEY

WHO PUT BELLA IN THE WYCH ELM?

It's a question that likely won't be answered. But as you drive through Worcestershire, past the dark, brooding woods of Hagley, you can't help but wonder. Somewhere, in a dusty attic or in a forgotten file, the answer might still be waiting.

But for now, Bella remains in the tree, the West Midlands' most famous, and most silent, resident.

THE GIRL IN THE BURNING CAR (OR, THE MAN IN THE BOWLER HAT)

Northumberland, 1931

The Northumberland moors in winter are not a landscape; they are a mood. They are vast, rolling waves of heather and bracken, turning black as the sun dips below the horizon. The wind cuts across them without obstruction, carrying the bite of the North Sea. It is a place of ancient beauty, but also of profound isolation. If you scream out here, the sound is swallowed by the silence before it travels ten yards.

On the night of January 6, 1931, that silence was broken by the roar of an engine and the crackle of flames. At a lonely spot known as Wolf's Nick, a name that sounds like a warning from a fairytale, a car was burning. And inside the inferno was a young woman who had committed the unforgivable sin of trying to be modern in a world that desperately wanted her to stay in her place.

Her name was Evelyn Foster. She was twenty-nine years old, and she was about to become the victim of two crimes: a savage murder by a stranger, and a character assassination by the state.

In 1931, a woman driving a car was a head-turner. A woman driving a taxi for a living was practically a revolutionary act. It made Evelyn a trailblazer. She worked for her father's hire-car business in Otterburn. She was skilled, independent, and fearless, traits that served her well on the winding country roads, but which would be used against her in death.

On that freezing Tuesday evening, she was at the wheel of her car, when she had picked up a fare in the village. The passenger was a man. He was described simply: respectable, well-dressed, wearing a dark overcoat and a bowler hat. He looked like a thousand other men in England. He asked to be driven to Ponteland, a journey of about twenty miles south.
Evelyn put the car in gear and drove him into the dark but she would never reach Ponteland.

What happened next comes to us from the only witness who mattered: Evelyn herself.

Hours later, a bus driver passing Wolf's Nick saw the glow. The car was now a burning torch against the night sky. The heat was intense, melting the glass and blistering the paint.

But the driver noticed something moving in the heather nearby.

It was Evelyn.

She had managed to crawl out of the burning wreckage. Her condition was horrific. Her clothes were burned away. Her skin was charred. She was in agony that defies description but her mind was lucid. She was desperate to speak, desperate to tell them what had happened? before the shock took her.

She told the rescuers, and later, her family and the police, a consistent, terrifying story.

The man in the bowler hat had attacked her. He hadn't wanted to go to Ponteland. He had forced her to stop on the moors. He had assaulted her, though in 1931, the details of sexual assault were often veiled in euphemism, but it's not a leap of logic to imagine what she injured.

When she resisted, and fought back with everything she had, he turned murderous. He poured petrol over the interior of the car. Then poured it over her. He locked her inside the car.
And then, with a callousness that chills the blood, he struck a match and walked away, leaving her to burn alive on the empty moor.

Evelyn Foster survived for twelve hours. She died in her own bed, surrounded by her family. Her final words were a plea for justice and a repetition of her account: The man. The bowler hat. The petrol.

The police launched a manhunt. They searched the moors. They checked the bus routes. They looked for a man smelling of smoke and petrol. A man with unexplained injuries as, by her own account, Evelyn had fought back.

But the man had vanished. The moors are vast, and a man walking alone in the dark is easily missed.

However, the real villain of this story arguably wasn't the man with the match. It was the man with the gavel.

The coroner in charge of the inquest was Sir Alfred

Appleby.

He was a man of his time, arrogant, patriarchal, and deeply suspicious of any woman who dared to step outside what he saw as their assigned roles.

He didn't like Evelyn's story. It was too dramatic. It featured a mysterious villain who couldn't be found. And, perhaps most unforgivably, it featured a young woman engaging in "man's work" alone at night.

Appleby began to spin a different narrative. He suggested that there was no man. He suggested that Evelyn had set fire to the car herself.

Why? Insurance fraud? A lover's tiff? A hysterical episode? He was of the firm belief that a woman, left alone in charge of a motorcar, would likely be reduced to hysterics. If that woman were driving a rural, windy road, at night? Then hysterics triggering a case of spontaneous human combustion brought about by stress and "women being women," was a distinct possibility.

He ignored the forensic evidence. He ignored the fact that she had fought her way out of a burning vehicle. He ignored her dying declaration, something usually considered the most truthful testimony in law, he let his own prejudices cloud his judgment and ignore every fact in the case.

Instead, he insinuated that she was a liar. He painted her as unstable. In his summation to the jury, he all but instructed them to return a verdict of suicide or accidental death. He wanted to tidy the mess up. He, like so many, wanted to blame the victim.

But the jury, twelve local men who knew the moors and perhaps knew the character of the Foster family, refused to be bullied.

They listened to Appleby's sneering summation before retiring to make their decision. When they returned, they delivered a verdict that was a direct slap in the face to the coroner.

"Wilful Murder by a Person or Persons Unknown."

They believed Evelyn.

Appleby was furious. He famously snapped at the jury, telling them their verdict was "against the weight of the evidence." But their decision stood. The people of Otterburn knew that Evelyn Foster hadn't burned herself alive. They knew a monster had walked their roads and had violently assaulted and killed one of their own.

And they sure as hell weren't going to let a sexist old coroner tell them otherwise.

Who was the man in the bowler hat? Theories abound. Some say he was a local man who had been obsessed with Evelyn. Others suggest he was a stranger passing through, a predator who saw a lone female driver, and seized an opportunity before being engulfed by rage.

There is a darker theory involving a similar attack in the area years later, suggesting a serial offender operating in the wilds of Northumberland—a "Wolf of the Moors" who hunted in the blind spots of the countryside.

But if such a serial killer existed? He was never caught.

A modern cynicism might question what really drove Sir Alfred Appleby to be so dismissive of the evidence. Could he have been attempting to use his power and influence to cover for the true perpetrator, perhaps someone he knew, or was related too? It's speculation but powerful men, covering up serious crimes for their friends, is a phenomenon as old as time itself. And something that still occurs with depressing regularity to this day.

The fire destroyed the car, and with it, any fingerprints or fibres. The wind blew away his footprints. He walked out of the firelight and back into the anonymity of the north.

The tragedy of Evelyn Foster fits perfectly into the noir landscape we have been exploring.

It has the setting: the desolate, wind-scoured north.

It has the mystery: the stranger in the hat.

It has the injustice: the establishment figure (Appleby) who preferred to destroy a woman's reputation rather than admit he couldn't solve the crime.

Evelyn Foster was a pioneer. She was doing a job she loved in an era that told her she shouldn't. She fought her attacker on the moors, and she fought to stay alive long enough to name the crime.

But history has been slow to forgive the coroner's smear. For decades, whispers persisted in the area—whispers started by Appleby—that perhaps she did do it to herself.

It wasn't until almost a century later that campaigns by her family and true crime historians finally cleared the smoke. We now see Evelyn not as the hysterical woman of Appleby's invention, but as the brave victim of a horrific crime.

If you drive past Wolf's Nick today, the road is quiet. The heather still grows thick and dark.

It is a beautiful place. But beauty can hide terrible things.
Somewhere on those moors, a man walked away with the smell of petrol on his hands. And somewhere in the archives of Newcastle, there is a record of a coroner who tried to burn Evelyn Foster a second time.

She survived the fire just long enough to tell the truth. It took the rest of the world ninety years to listen.

THE SAINT IN THE DANCE HALL (OR, SATURDAY NIGHT FEVER WITH A VENGEANCE)

Glasgow, The late 1960s

If you were young, single, and living in Glasgow in the late 1960s, there was really only one place to be on a Saturday night: The Barrowland Ballroom.

It was a cavernous, neon-lit cathedral of courtship located in the Gallowgate. It was the sort of place where the air smelled of stale cigarette smoke, Old Spice, and just the faintest hint of desperation. The floor was sprung to bounce under the weight of a thousand jiving couples, and the rules were simple: the men stood on one side, the women on the other, and at a predetermined signal, the two armies would advance to engage in the ritualistic combat known as "the lumber."

For the uninitiated, "to lumber" in Glaswegian parlance means to successfully pick up a partner. It is a word that implies heavy lifting, which, given the alcohol consumption involved, was often accurate.

But between 1968 and 1969, the Barrowland Ballroom stopped being just a place to find a fling. It became the hunting ground for Scotland's most notorious, and most sanctimonious, serial killer.

He was a man who didn't fit the profile. He wasn't a shadowy lurking creep; he was polite. He was well-dressed. He didn't slur his words. And, most curiously of all, he really, really liked the Old Testament.

They called him Bible John. And if Jack the Ripper was the Victorian embodiment of the "mad slasher," Bible John was the uniquely Scottish nightmare of the "judgmental kirk elder."

The terror began in February 1968 with Patricia Docker. Patricia was a 25-year-old nurse, a mother, and by all accounts, a woman just looking for a night off. She went to the Barrowland, danced the night away, and left early as she was hoping to catch a bus home to Langside.

She never made it. Her body was found the next morning in a doorway, just yards from her home. She had been strangled.

At the time, the police treated it as a tragic, but isolated, incident. Glasgow was a tough city and bad things occasionally happened. The investigation was hampered by the fact that Patricia's clothes and handbag were missing. Without identification, it took days to figure out who she was. By then, the trail was colder than a bleak midwinter in the Highlands.

When she was identified the pace picked up, 700 taxi drivers were interviewed, and a manhunt was put in place for the owner of a Morris 1000. A woman was seen getting into it before it sped off out into the night. The driver was never located. However, the occupants of another car spotted acting suspiciously, did come forward. It was a couple using the backseat to conduct their illicit affair.

When the leads ran dry, the city moved on, and the dancing continued. Then, on Saturday, August 16th, 1969, Jemima McDonald, a 32-year-old mother of three, went to the Barrowland. She was a regular, known for her love of a good night out.

She met a man. Witnesses described him as tall, slim, and sporting the kind of reddish-fair hair that looks charming in a certain light and soulless in another. They left the ballroom together.

Jemima wasn't found until the following Monday. Her sister, Margaret O'Brien, concerned that Jemima hadn't returned home, began to search the area herself.

She overheard several local children talking about finding a body in an old derelict tenement, wondering if they should tell someone, or if they'd be in trouble for trespassing. As she listened, a sense of dread building inside her, the lads decided they were far more afraid of their mothers anger, so opted to remain quiet.

She persuaded them to tell her where they'd seen the body, promising not to tell their mums. This led to a scene that no family member should ever have to endure. She walked into the derelict tenement building near their home, and it was there that she found her sister.

Jemima had been strangled with her own stockings. She was fully clothed, but her handbag was missing.

Now, the police began to sweat. Two women. Both met at the Barrowland. Both strangled near their homes. Both were robbed of their handbags. The press began to sniff around, sensing that this wasn't just random violence, this was a pattern.

But the killer wasn't done yet.

The case of Bible John hinges almost entirely on the events of October 31, 1969. It is one of the most vividly detailed encounters with a serial killer in history where the witness survived to tell the tale.

Helen Puttock, 29, went to the Barrowland with her sister, Jean. They were having a good night. They met two men. One was named "Castlemilk John" (because in Glasgow, your nickname is usually just your name plus the housing estate you live in). The other was a tall, smart-looking man who introduced himself simply as "John."

Castlemilk John was harmless. He walked to the bus stop and vanished from the story. The other John, however, offered to share a taxi with the sisters.

It is this taxi ride that created the legend.

For roughly an hour, Jean sat in a confined space with the man who would murder her sister. And the man could not stop talking. But he wasn't chatting about the football scores or the weather. He was talking about morality.

He asked the women if they were married. They both were, but they didn't wear their rings to the dance hall, a common practice to avoid scaring off potential dance partners. John was not amused. He launched into a lecture about the sanctity of marriage. He called the Barrowland an "adulterous den of iniquity."

He then dropped the quote that would give him his name. When the conversation turned to religion, he referenced stories from the Bible with the confidence of a Sunday School teacher gone rogue. He mentioned Moses. He talked about "holes," specifically in golf courses, and at one point, he said: "I don't drink at Hogmanay. I pray."

Now, to an outsider, this might sound merely pious. To a Glaswegian, a man who doesn't drink at Hogmanay (New Year's Eve) is immediately suspicious. It indicates a level of restraint that borders on the psychopathic.

The taxi dropped Jean off at her home first. She said goodnight to her sister and the polite, scripture-quoting man. It was the last time she saw Helen alive.

Helen's body was found the next morning in the back garden of her Earl Street flat. She had been strangled. Her handbag was missing. And, significantly, grass stains on her feet suggested a struggle.

The police now had a description that was almost too good to be true. Jean had spent an hour with him. She described him as:

* Tall and slim.

* Reddish hair, neatly cut.

* Overlapping front teeth (the kind, apparently, that give you a slightly predatory rabbit look).

* Dressed in a smart suit, possibly from a tailor like "Burton's."

The police released a composite sketch, the first time the City of Glasgow force has ever done so, and it showed a man with a sharp face and a fashionable haircut. It became one of the most famous images in Scotland.

The investigation that followed was frantic. It was the biggest manhunt Scotland had ever seen. They interviewed 50,000 men. They took 5,000 statements.

But the methods used were... let's call them "of their time." Desperate to catch the killer, the police decided that the best way to find a man who frequents dance halls was to go in dancing. Undercover officers were deployed to the Barrowland as well as other local night spots.

Picture this: grizzled Glasgow detectives, men who spent their days dealing with petty crime and hardened criminals, suddenly had to learn to Jive. They were given haircuts to look younger, which unfortunately made them look like old men with bad haircuts. They stood on the edge of the dance floor, awkwardly sipping warm beer, eyeing up anyone with red hair and bad teeth.

Unsurprisingly, "Bible John" did not approach an undercover policeman and ask for the last waltz. They even issued all male dancers a small card, a sort of "I've been checked" pass. If you didn't have your card, you were a suspect. It turned the Saturday night "lumber" into a bureaucratic exercise.

The Theories: Who was he?

So, who was this man who could quote Leviticus while committing murder?

Theory 1: The Policeman

One persistent rumour was that John was a cop. He showed a flash of an ID card to the taxi driver (though this was disputed). He knew how to strangle quickly and cleanly. And, crucially, he seemed to vanish into thin air, perhaps because he knew exactly how the police operated. It's a classic trope, but in the tight-knit world of 1960s Glasgow policing, could they have covered up for one of their own? Unlikely, but it made for good pub gossip.

Theory 2: The Soldier

The "smart haircut" and the politeness screamed military. Glasgow was full of servicemen on leave. Had he come home, killed, and then shipped out before the photofit hit the papers?

Theory 3: Peter Tobin (The Modern Monster)

This is where the story gets truly dark. For decades, Bible John was a ghost. But in the 2000s, a man named Peter Tobin was convicted of the brutal murders of Angelika Kluk, Vicky Hamilton, and Dinah McNicol.

Tobin was a monster. He operated in the 60s. He lived in Glasgow. He was a serial killer who raped and murdered young women.

When police looked at young Peter Tobin, the resemblance to the Bible John sketch was chilling. The overlapping teeth? Check. The height? Check.

More damningly, Tobin had aliases. He had moved to Brighton shortly after the murders stopped (Bible John reportedly told Jean he came from the south or moved around). Tobin was a churchgoer.

Many criminologists are now convinced that Bible John was simply Peter Tobin in his early years, practising his craft before he became the drifter killer of the 2000s. Tobin died in 2022, refusing to confess to the Bible John murders. If he was the man, he took the satisfaction of the secret to the grave.

It's also worth considering that there might be other victims. Over half a dozen young women who fitted the victim profile, slim, "attractive," and brunette, vanished in the late 1960s; only these poor women were never found.

Could they have been further victims of Bible John? Victims whose remains have remained hidden to this day? It's a terrifying prospect.

Bible John wasn't the only monster stalking the streets of Glasgow in the late 1960s. As we've seen, Peter Tobin, who police officially believed was not Bible John, was in the city at the time. If Tobin and John weren't the same man it meant that there was a third serial killer stalking Glasgow's streets at the time: Fred West. Arguably the most notorious British serial killer of them all who, along with his wife Rose, killed at least a dozen young women.

The first death confirmed to be at West's hands happened in Glasgow. The ice cream van he was driving hit a young lad, just three years old. The police said it was a freak accident. The locals believed otherwise and Fred was essentially forced to flee Glasgow.

He also kept an allotment at the time, and was known to constantly be digging there, yet nothing ever grew. If he did have a hand involved in the disappearances, the truth now lies buried, underneath a major motorway junction.

The Bible John murders stopped as abruptly as they began. Perhaps he moved. Perhaps he was jailed for something else. Perhaps he simply grew out of it, though serial killers rarely just "retire," as to many it's a form of dark compulsion.

But the legacy remained. For a generation of Glasgow women, the Barrowland was no longer just a dance hall; it was a risk assessment. The image of the red-haired man haunted the city.

There is a grim irony in the moniker "Bible John." The killer used scripture to berate his victims for their "loose morals," for dancing, for enjoying life. He positioned himself as a moral arbiter, a hand of God acting in the sinful city.

In reality, he was a petty, angry man who hated women. He didn't kill them because of the Bible; ultimately, he killed them because he could.

Today, the Barrowland is a famous concert venue. Rock bands play where the orchestras once swung. The ghost of Bible John has faded, replaced by the noise of guitars and cheering crowds.

But if you ask a Glaswegian of a certain age, they remember. They remember the sketch. They remember the fear. And they remember the golden rule of the late 1960s: If a handsome stranger in a suit asks you to share a taxi, and starts quoting Moses…

Get out and walk.

THE LEFT LUGGAGE (OR, THE GIRL WITH THE DANCER'S LEGS)

Brighton, 1934

In the 1930s, Brighton was "London by the Sea." It was the place where the capital loosened its tie, rolled up its trousers, and breathed in the salt air. It was a town of piers, pierrots, sticks of rock, and illicit weekends.

But Brighton has always had a shadow. Behind the Regency facades and the tea rooms lay a network of boarding houses, back alleys, and transient souls. It was a place where people went to disappear, or to reinvent themselves, or, as it turned out in the summer of 1934, to be disposed of.

On June 17th, 1934, the shadow fell across Brighton Railway Station. The heat was rising. The station was busy with holidaymakers. But in the left-luggage office, the staff were dealing with a problem that no amount of sea breeze could shift.

There was a smell and it was coming from a plywood trunk that had been deposited there almost two weeks earlier, on June 6th. The smell was sweet, cloying, and unmistakable to anyone who had served in the Great War.

Eventually, the Chief Constable was called and the trunk was opened. Inside, wrapped in brown paper and cotton wool, was the torso of a woman.

The discovery set off one of the biggest police operations in British history. Scotland Yard was called in. The station was swarmed.

But the trunk offered more questions than answers. The victim had been dismembered with surgical, almost butcher-like precision. The killer had removed the head, the arms, and the legs. All that remained was the torso.

The police were left with a biological puzzle. Pathologists determined she was around twenty-five years old. She was healthy. And, crucially, her feet, which were later found in a separate suitcase at King's Cross Station in London, suggested she was a dancer. They were well-cared-for, with the distinctive muscle structure of someone who spent a lot of time on her toes.

The press, always eager for a hook, dubbed her "The Girl with the Dancer's Legs." But who was she?

Thousands of women were reported missing at the time. Police checked lists, interviewed landladies, and combed the dance halls of the south coast. They reconstructed her potential height. They guessed at her weight.

But the Girl in the Trunk had no name. She had no family coming forward. She was a mystery, and most shockingly of all? She wasn't alone.

The police began a house-to-house search of the areas near the station, looking for anyone who might have seen the trunk being moved. They knocked on a door in Kemp Street, a rundown terrace in the North Laine district. The house was a warren of bedsits. One of the residents was a twenty-six-year-old waiter and petty thief named Tony Mancini.

Mancini was nervous. He told the police he had nothing to hide. But when they left, he didn't wait around. He packed his bags and fled to London. The police, suspicious of his flight, returned to Kemp Street, where they searched his room.

At the foot of his bed, serving as a coffee table, was a black trunk. They opened it.

Inside was the decomposing body of a woman.

This time, she was whole. This time, she had a name. She was Violette Kaye, a forty-two-year-old dancer and prostitute who had been Mancini's lover. She had been missing since May.

The police thought they had cracked it. Two trunks. Two bodies. One suspect. It seemed like an open-and-shut case of a serial killer operating in the boarding houses of Brighton.

They hunted Mancini down. He was arrested near London and brought back to face trial. The narrative was simple: Mancini had killed his girlfriend, Violette Kaye, in a fit of rage or greed. And, the police assumed, he had

also killed the unknown woman found at the station.

But here is where the story twists.

Mancini was charged only with the murder of Violette Kaye. The police didn't have enough evidence to link him to the first victim. They hoped that a conviction for one would be enough to hang him for both.

At the trial in Lewes Assizes, Mancini's defence team pulled off a miracle. Mancini admitted he had hidden Violette's body. He admitted he had lied. But he claimed he hadn't killed her. He said he came home and found her dead, a victim of a drug overdose or natural causes.

Panicked, and knowing his criminal record would make him the prime suspect, he hid her in the trunk to buy time.

"I am not a murderer," he told the court. "I am a man who was afraid."

The jury believed him.

In a verdict that stunned the nation, Tony Mancini was found Not Guilty. He walked out of the court a free man.

For forty years, Mancini lived with the secret. But the truth has a way of rising to the surface, much like a body in water.

In 1976, dying and desperate for attention, Mancini spoke to a journalist. He confessed to killing Violette Kaye. They had argued. He had thrown a hammer at her. It had struck her temple. He had watched her die, then stuffed her into the trunk and lived with the corpse in his bedroom for weeks, using it as a table, sleeping inches away from his victim.

He had played the jury like a fiddle. But, and this is the crucial part, Mancini went to his grave denying any knowledge of the first trunk.

"I killed Violette," he insisted. "But I never touched the other girl."

So, who killed the Girl with the Dancer's Legs?

If we believe Mancini, and deathbed confessions usually carry some weight regarding what one didn't do, then there were two killers operating in Brighton in the summer of 1934.

Two killers using trunks to dispose of their victims. Trunks ultimately found within a mile of each other.

It seems like an impossible coincidence. And yet, the details don't match.

Violette Kaye was killed with a hammer and stuffed into a trunk, whole. It was messy, panicked, and crude.

The first victim was dismembered with skill. The joints were unarticulated cleanly. The blood had been drained. It spoke of a cold, clinical efficiency that Mancini, a petty thief and hothead, didn't seem to possess.

Was there a second monster in Brighton that summer?

Some theories point to a local doctor or a butcher, someone with anatomical knowledge. Others suggest the first trunk came down from London on the train, meaning the killer might not have been in Brighton at all. The trunk was simply the delivery method; the station was the dumping ground.

The Brighton Trunk Murders exposed the dark side of the seaside dream.

Brighton was a place of transience. People came for the weekend. They checked into boarding houses under false names. They had affairs. They drifted.

The first victim was likely one of these drifters. She might have been pregnant (a common motive for "medical" murders of the time). She might have been a runaway.

Because she was never identified, she remains the ultimate victim. She is not a person; she is "The Body at the Station." Her entire existence has been reduced to a piece of luggage left on a shelf.

Today, Brighton Station is a cathedral of glass and steel, filled with commuters and coffee shops. The left-luggage office is gone.

But the story remains lodged in the city's folklore. It reminds us that anonymity is dangerous. In a city of strangers, you can disappear, and no one will ask where you went until the smell becomes impossible to ignore.

Tony Mancini got away with murder for forty years. The killer of the first girl looks to have gotten away with it forever.

And somewhere in an unmarked grave, the Girl with the Dancer's Legs lies waiting for a name that will likely never come. The trunk containing her torso was opened, but the mystery surrounding who she was, what she was called, remains locked tight.

THE MAN WHO DIDN'T DO IT (OR, THE SCOTTISH DREYFUSS)

Glasgow, 1908

In 1908, Glasgow was the Second City of the Empire. It was a powerhouse of shipbuilding, heavy industry, and smoke. It was a city of hard men and harder fortunes, where the soot from the chimneys coated the lungs of the poor and the sandstone facades of the rich alike.

It was a city that prided itself on its Victorian morality. It liked order. It liked propriety. And, as it turned out, it really, really disliked foreigners.

This prejudice would become the fuel for one of the most scandalous miscarriages of justice in British legal history. The case of Oscar Slater isn't just a murder mystery; it's a story about what happens when a city decides that finding a scapegoat is more important than finding the truth.

Marion Gilchrist was eighty-two years old. She was wealthy, she was a spinster, and she was terrified. She lived in a first-floor flat at 15 West Princes Street, a respectable address in the West End. Her apartment was a fortress. She had double locks on the doors. She had a patent lock on the back window. She had a pre-arranged signal with the neighbours. If she knocked on the floor three times, it meant trouble.

She lived with her jewels—a collection worth

thousands of pounds—hidden in her wardrobe. She lived with her fear. And she lived with her servant, a twenty-one-year-old girl named Helen Lambie.

On the evening of December 21, 1908, the fortress was breached. Around 7:00 p.m., Helen Lambie popped out to buy a newspaper. She was gone for ten minutes. In those ten minutes, the neighbour below, Arthur Adams, heard a noise. It wasn't the three knocks. It was a heavy thud, followed by the sound of something breaking.

Adams, a concerned citizen, went upstairs. He rang the bell. No answer. He heard the sound of paper being torn. He waited. When Helen Lambie returned, keys in hand, they opened the door together.

As the door opened, a man walked out of the bedroom. He didn't run. He didn't scream. He walked past the servant and the neighbour with a cool, oddly pleasant, demeanour. It was only when he reached the stairs that he accelerated, bolting down the steps and vanishing into the gaslit fog of the Glasgow night.

Inside the bedroom, they found Marion Gilchrist, beaten to death. Her head had been smashed in, her face unrecognisable. A chair had been used to strike her, as well as a heavy hammer-like object. A rug had been thrown crudely over her body.

The room was ransacked, papers were scattered everywhere, which was likely the tearing sound Adams had heard.

But here is the detail that should have stopped the police in their tracks. Despite the thousands of pounds worth of jewellery in the wardrobe, only one piece was missing: A single diamond crescent brooch.

The Glasgow Police were under pressure. A rich old lady

bludgeoned in the West End? The public demanded a hanging, but they had a problem. The killer seemed to know the layout. There was no forced entry. The "three knocks" signal hadn't been used. It smacked of an inside job, or at least someone the victim knew.

But the police didn't want an inside job, and they certainly didn't want to look at the victim's family, who stood to inherit her fortune. They wanted a monster so they found one: Oscar Slater.

Slater was everything Edwardian Glasgow feared. He was German. He was Jewish. He was a gambler. He lived with a woman he wasn't married to, a French entertainer, no less. He allegedly lived off the proceeds of prostitution, though this was never proven, but the allegation at the time was enough. He wore flashy clothes, dressing flamboyantly in an era where this made one stand out, and most damning of all to the detectives on the case? He was known for using aliases.

He was the perfect "Other."

The police caught wind that Slater had been trying to pawn a pawn ticket for a diamond brooch. Their eyes lit up, and they went "Bingo!"

It didn't matter that Slater had pawned the brooch weeks before the murder. It didn't matter that it was confirmed to be his own brooch. It didn't matter that he had practically announced his departure for America days before the crime, he was chasing new gambling opportunities, not fleeing justice. The police had their narrative. The foreigner killed the lady for her jewels.

Slater boarded the Lusitania for New York. The police framed it as a desperate flight from the law. They cabled New York, turning it into an international manhunt, and the fact that he couldn't physically have killed Marion and made it for his crossing? That didn't matter.

When Slater arrived in America, he was immediately arrested, and he was baffled. He voluntarily agreed to return to Scotland to clear his name, believing that the British justice system would surely see that he had nothing to do with it, but he underestimated how much Glasgow wanted him to be guilty.

The key witnesses, the servant girl Helen Lambie and the neighbour Arthur Adams, were brought to New York to identify him. It's a surreal story – the two people closest to Marion being bundled on a transatlantic sailing just a day after her murder.

Before the line-up, they were reportedly shown Slater in handcuffs. They were told, "That's the man." Unsurprisingly, when asked to identify him, they pointed to Slater. If you'd just been told by a police officer that this is, beyond all doubt, the culprit – would you also trust them and point to the man indicated?

Back in Glasgow, the trial was nothing short of a circus. The Lord Advocate (the prosecutor) didn't focus on evidence; he focused on character assassination. He painted Slater as a pimp, a degenerate, a man of "low morals." The implication was clear: If he's bad enough to live in sin, then surely he's bad enough to bash someone's head in. A wrong un is a wrong un - what further proof was needed?

Slater's alibi was solid, he was having dinner on the other side of the city, waiting to board his ship. The witnesses were his "immoral" friends, so they were ignored, their testimony tainted by living a lifestyle frowned upon by society at the time. The alibi was so strong that, for Slater to have committed the crime and still make his crossing, he'd have needed to travel

70mph across the city at a time when that wasn't possible.

In May 1909, the jury returned a verdict, guilty, by a majority of nine to six, and Slater was sentenced to death. He was to be hanged at Duke Street Prison. But the case smelt of a miscarriage of justice. The press, the public, and even many within the legal system noticed it and murmurs about a retrial began.

Two days before the execution, the sentence was commuted to life imprisonment with hard labour. Why? If he was a cold-blooded killer, hang him. If there was doubt, free him. Commuting the sentence suggested the authorities knew the conviction was shaky, they didn't want a man's blood on their hands, but they also couldn't bear to admit they were wrong.

Slater went to Peterhead Prison, a grim fortress on the cliffs of the North Sea, and he would stay there for eighteen and a half years.

The man who eventually saved Oscar Slater wasn't a lawyer nor a judge. It was one of the most famous men in the country: Arthur Conan Doyle.

The creator of Sherlock Holmes took an interest in the case. He applied his own detective's eye to the files, relishing the chance to act out a case as his famous creation, and he spotted the holes immediately.

* The hammer found in Slater's trunk was too light to cause the injuries. It was a toffee hammer, the kind found in Christmas Crackers, a mere inch in size.

* The brooch used as evidence was the wrong brooch. This mattered as it was impossible, without the aid of a Time Machine, to pawn a stolen brooch weeks before its theft.

* The witnesses had been coached. Being told, definitively, that he was guilty and that they needed to point to him as "a formality"

* The killer walked out of the flat calmly—suggesting he knew he wouldn't be recognized as a stranger, or that he had the arrogance of someone who belonged there.

Conan Doyle wrote a book, The Case of Oscar Slater, dismantling the prosecution. He campaigned for years and called it a stain on Scottish justice.

It took until 1927 for the pressure to finally break. A secret message smuggled out of prison by Slater reached the press. The outcry was deafening.

Slater was released. He was awarded £6,000 in compensation, a fortune then, but a pittance for eighteen years of hell.

So, if Oscar Slater didn't murder Marion Gilchrist, who did?

The theories point uncomfortably close to home.

Many historians believe the killer was a relative of Marion Gilchrist, specifically, a nephew who was desperate for money.

This explains the lack of forced entry. She opened the door to him. It explains the violence; a family argument gone wrong. It explains why only one brooch was taken. It was a staged theft to look like a burglary, but the killer panicked. A family member would also have known if one brooch in particular could have been worth more than the rest of the collection, combined.

It explains why the man walked out calmly past the neighbour. He knew he looked like a gentleman, not a burglar.

Most damningly of all, it explained the police behaviour. In 1908, the Glasgow police would much rather hang a "dirty foreigner," than arrest a respectable member of the Scottish middle class. They protected their own by sacrificing everyone else.

Oscar Slater died in 1948. By the end he was a bitter, difficult man, and who could blame him?

The murder of Marion Gilchrist remains officially unsolved. But it is solved in an important way: we know who didn't do it. And, although it took 18 years, an injustice was corrected. This chapter could so easily have been the tale of two people's unjust deaths. Wrongful verdicts, resulting in innocent men hanging for crimes they didn't commit, were a lot more common than we'd like to admit.

Better to leave a guilty man to rot in prison for a lifetime than to risk the wrongful death of an innocent man.

THE MAN WITHOUT A NAME (OR, THE HARVEST OF BONE)

Lincolnshire, 1974

In the balmy summer of 1974, Lincolnshire was a place of deceptive simplicity.

It is a county of big skies and low horizons, where the land runs flat and hard toward the North Sea. The roads are straight, cutting through miles of cabbage fields and sugar beet, bordered by deep, silt-clogged ditches and dykes. It is a landscape that feels open, exposed, and honest. You can stand on a fenland road and see for miles in every direction.

But openness is not the same as transparency. The very vastness of the place offers a different kind of cover. If you want to hide something in a city, you bury it in the noise. If you want to hide something in rural Lincolnshire, you bury it in the silence.

It was in this quiet, agricultural stillness that the county began to yield a grim harvest. It didn't produce crops; it produced a man, piece by mutilated piece.

The nightmare didn't begin with a scream or a dramatic confession. It began with the mundane.

In 1974, a member of the public, someone walking a dog, or perhaps a farmhand checking a fence, noticed something out of place near Grimsby. It was just a shape in the grass, something pale against the green. It was enough to make them call the police, and when they arrived, the reality of the find shattered the rural peace. It was human remains. But it wasn't a body; it was only a part of one.

The discovery was clinical and horrifying. This wasn't a death by natural causes, a heart attack on a country stroll. This was a deliberate act of disassembly. The police cordoned off the area. They searched the dykes and the hedgerows. And soon, the terrible truth became clear: this wasn't the only site.

As the inquiry widened, reports began to come in from other locations across the county. Parts were found near Peartree Way. Others surfaced in different isolated spots across the length and breadth of Lincolnshire.

The realisation was chilling. The killer hadn't just dumped the body in a panic. He had distributed it, methodically, piece by piece.

This is where the profile of the killer begins to emerge from the landscape itself. Panic usually looks like a shallow grave or a body dumped in a river. But this? This was different.

The dismemberment suggested a cold practicality. But the scattering suggested something else: local knowledge. Whoever did this must have known the back roads of Lincolnshire like the back of their hand. They knew which lanes were quiet at night. They knew which ditches were overgrown enough to hold a secret for a few days.

It implied a vehicle. It implied time. And it implied a terrifying degree of confidence. To drive around a county with human remains in the boot of your car requires a nerve that most people simply do not possess. The killer used the countryside as a filing cabinet, slotting pieces of evidence into the landscape, perhaps where they hoped they would never be found.

They were almost right. The police found the remains, but they never found the man. The investigation hit a wall almost immediately, and it was a wall that no amount of detective work could scale. They didn't know who he was.

Usually, a murder investigation starts with the victim. You look at their life. Who were their enemies? Who owed them money? Who was sleeping with their wife? You build a picture of the dead to find the living.

But here, there was no picture.

There were no missing person reports that matched the description. No frantic wife or parents came forward to identify a jagged scar or a birthmark. No clothing was found that could offer a label or a laundry mark.

The victim was a blank slate. He was a biological male, age indeterminate but adult, height estimated, weight estimated. He was a collection of statistics.

In death, he had achieved the ultimate anonymity. And without a name, the police were chasing a phantom.

As it stands it looks likely that he will never be identified. It has been over half a century so it's now equally likely that his killer will never be caught. He has become a ghost story told in police canteens, a file that grew yellow and brittle with age. He was transformed from a human being with a history, a family, and a name, into a series of biological exhibits.

To understand the frustration of the Lincolnshire police, you have to look at the toolkit they were working with.

Today, a case like this would be blown open by science. We would have DNA profiling. We would have familial

DNA searches that could link the victim to a distant cousin in a different country. We would have CCTV of the killer's car. We would have mobile phone tower data placing the victim and the killer at the same spot.

In 1974, they had none of that.

Forensic science was analogue. Pathologists could look at the bones and tell you it was a man. They could tell you he had been killed before he was cut up (a small mercy). They could tell you the tool used was likely a saw.

But they couldn't tell you his name. Dental records, the usual backup for identification, are useless if you don't know which dentist to call. They're even more useless if, like in this case, you never find the head. Blood grouping is a broad brush; it's often more useful for telling you who the victim isn't, rather than who they are.

The man remained a puzzle with half the pieces missing. One big question is simply this: why was he never missed?

This brings us to Grimsby itself. In the mid-1970s, Grimsby was a hard-working, hard-drinking town defined by the sea. The fishing industry was still the beating heart of the economy, though the first murmurs of the cod wars and industrial decline were beginning to be felt.

It was a transient town. Trawlers went out for weeks at a time. Men came from all over the country to work the docks. They stayed in cheap boarding houses, drank away their pay, and moved on. It was a place where faces changed like the tides.

If a man disappeared from a lodging house in Grimsby, people didn't assume he was dead. They assumed he'd shipped out. They assumed he'd gone back to Liverpool, or Hull, or London. They assumed he'd run from a debt or a woman. That was a story so common, it applied to hundreds, and it gave an excuse to look the other way.

The victim likely lived on these margins. He was perhaps a seasonal worker, an itinerant labourer, or someone estranged from his family. He was one of the "unsettled"—the people who fall through the cracks of society while they are alive, and slip through them entirely when they are dead.

While the victim remains a mystery, the killer is a spectre that haunts the case.

The police knew one thing for certain: the dismemberment happened after death. This matters. It suggested to them that the mutilation wasn't sexual or ritualistic; it was pragmatic. It was done to conceal the crime and to make the evidence easier to conceal.

By removing the head and hands (often the first parts to be hidden in such cases), the killer strips the victim of identity. No face. No fingerprints. The head and hands have, to date, never been found.

This implies a relationship. You don't usually go to the trouble of dismembering a stranger you robbed in an alley. You dismember someone who can be linked to you. You dismember someone whose identification would lead the police directly to your door.

The killer was likely someone the victim knew. Someone who had a house, a garage, or a workshop where they could undertake the gruesome task of separation without being heard or seen.

And they got away with it. Could they have stayed in Lincolnshire? If so they might have driven past the police cordons on their way to work. They might be alive today, assuming they were in their 20s at the time of the crime, they'd be in the mid to late 70s now. They could be watching the news, reading this book even, safe in the knowledge that their secret was safely buried in the files of the 1970s.

The case attracted a flurry of media attention. "Torso Mysteries" always do. They carry a Victorian, Jack-the-Ripper frisson, that sells newspapers.

But the public has a short attention span. Without a name, the victim couldn't be humanised. He wasn't "John, the father of two," or "David, the amateur footballer." He was just "The Body without a Head."

When no leads appeared, the journalists packed up their typewriters and went home. The case slipped from the front page, and then out of the news entirely.

There is a profound sadness in the "unclaimed dead." Without a name, there is no proper funeral. There is no grave marker. There is no anniversary. The victim exists only in the professional memory of the police officers who failed to close the case.

Today, the fields of Lincolnshire look much the same as they did in 1974. The crops rotate, the seasons turn, and the roads are resurfaced. New housing estates have encroached on the edges of Grimsby, covering the old waste grounds.

Life has layered itself over the crime.

But the mystery remains. The Grimsby Torso case is a stark reminder of the fragility of identity. We spend our lives building a name, a reputation, a history. But it takes surprisingly little to erase it all. To reduce us to nothing more than human meat in a field.

We will likely never know who the man was. We will

likely never know why he died. And we will likely never know who killed him.

All that remains is the geography. A ditch here, a hedgerow there. The landscape swallowed him twice: once when the pieces of him were being hidden, and again, when he was forgotten and left nameless.

In the end, this isn't just a story about a murder. It is a story about silence. The silence of the victim, the silence of the killer, and the silence of a county that holds its secrets in the deep, dark earth.

THE GIRL ON THE SHORE (OR, THE SILENCE OF LEITH)

Edinburgh, 1983

Edinburgh is a city of split personalities. It is the city of Dr. Jekyll and Mr. Hyde, quite literally, Robert Louis Stevenson wrote the book in the city, inspired by the dual nature of the place.

On one side, you have the Edinburgh of the tourist postcards: the Castle on the rock, the Georgian elegance of the New Town, the intellect of the Enlightenment, the Festival fireworks. It is a city of lawyers, academics, and old money. But if you walk down the hill, away from the polite crescents and towards the water, you find the other Edinburgh.

In 1983, Leith wasn't the trendy waterfront district it is today. There were no Michelin-star restaurants serving tasting menus. There were no converted loft apartments for graphic designers. Leith was rough. It was the port. It was industrial, scarred by poverty, and struggling to breathe under the weight of the heroin epidemic that would later be immortalised in Trainspotting.

It was here, in the shadow of the cranes and the gasworks, that a twenty-seven-year-old woman named Sheila Anderson lived, worked, and ultimately died. And it was here where Edinburgh demonstrated how little it cared about a woman who lived her life on the margins.

Sheila Anderson was a mother of two. She was described by those who knew her as quiet, fragile, and fiercely loving of her children. But in the eyes of the Lothian and Borders Police, she was defined by one thing only: she was a "working girl."

Sheila worked the beat on Commercial Street in Leith. It was a bleak, wind-battered stretch of road where women waited for cars to slow down, trading safety for survival.

On the night of April 7, 1983, Sheila was out working. It was a Thursday. The wind was coming off the Firth of Forth, cutting through coats and skin, leaving an icy chill in the spring air. Around 11:30 p.m., she was seen speaking to the driver of a white Rover.

She got into the car and it was the last time she was seen alive. Her body was found the next day at Gypsy Brae. If you don't know Edinburgh, Gypsy Brae sounds almost romantic. It isn't. It is a stretch of desolate foreshore in Granton, a wasteland of scrub grass and industrial debris looking out over the grey water of the Forth. It is a place where the city ends and the nothingness beyond starts.

The violence inflicted on Sheila was catastrophic. She hadn't just been beaten; she had been run over. The killer had used his vehicle as a weapon, driving over her repeatedly, crushing her into the gravel and mud. It was an act of rage that went far beyond the transaction of sex or robbery. It was an attempt to erase her.

The police arrived. The cordon went up. But the investigation that followed would be shaped, and ultimately doomed, by the prejudices of the time. In 1983, the term "High Risk Lifestyle" was police code for "Not a Priority."

When a sex worker was murdered, the unspoken assumption was often that it was an occupational hazard. The Yorkshire Ripper investigation, just a few years earlier, had highlighted this attitude on a national scale, where victims were categorised as "innocent" or "prostitutes," as if the latter group were somehow undeserving of justice. Sadly, Edinburgh proved to be no different.

The investigation into Sheila's death was sluggish. There was no immediate, city-wide panic. There were no warnings issued to "respectable" women to stay indoors, because the authorities believed the danger was confined to the red-light district, and this apathy gave the killer a head start. While the police were busy judging the victim's life, the man who ended it was likely washing his car, burning his clothes, then driving home to his family.

There was, briefly, a flicker of high-profile interest. Although Peter Sutcliffe, the Yorkshire Ripper, had been jailed in 1981, his shadow still loomed large over Britain. The brutality of Sheila's murder, the overkill, the targeting of a sex worker, mimicked his modus operandi.

Conspiracy theories swirled. Did the Ripper have an accomplice? Was this a copycat? Had Sutcliffe travelled to Scotland before his arrest and inspired a local disciple? The police looked into it. They checked files. They compared notes but the notion was a dead end. Sutcliffe was behind bars, and there was no evidence of a copycat ring, nor of any "disciples."

The focus on the "Ripper" angle was, in many ways, a distraction. It allowed the city to imagine that the evil was imported, a monster from the south, a mythical boogeyman. It was harder to accept the truth: that the killer was likely a local man, someone who knew the roads of Leith, someone who drove a white Rover and spoke with a Scots accent.

The car became the central clue. Witnesses had seen a white Rover SD1 in the area. It was a distinctive car, heavy, executive, the kind of vehicle driven by a manager or a salesman. By a man of means.

Police traced thousands of white Rovers. They stopped drivers. They set up roadblocks on Commercial Street. But a car is anonymous. In the dark, under the orange street lights of 1980s Leith, one white saloon looks much like another. Was it the killer's car? Or just a punter passing through? And was the car sighted that night even a white Rover to begin with?

A suspect did emerge, a local pimp and drug dealer, known to be violent. He was arrested, questioned, and even brought to trial years later in a cold case review. But the evidence wasn't there. The DNA was degraded or non-existent, as when Sheila was murdered DNA was still only a theoretical idea in a laboratory in Leicester. The witnesses were unreliable or dead.

The case collapsed.

To understand why Sheila's murder went unsolved, you have to look at the context of Edinburgh in the early 80s.

The city was in the grip of a heroin epidemic that gave it the unwanted title of the "AIDS capital of Europe." Leith was the epicentre. It was a community under siege, not just from poverty, but from a virus that was terrifying and deeply misunderstood.

In this climate, trust in the police was non-existent. The women working Commercial Street weren't going to talk to the cops. The addicts in the housing schemes weren't going to come forward as witnesses. There was a code of silence, born both out of fear, and also out of necessity.

The killer operated in this silence. He picked a victim who lived in the shadows, took her to a place where no one ventured at night, and left her where the tide washed away much of the evidence.

Today, Gypsy Brae is a place for dog walkers and cyclists. The industrial grime has been scrubbed away. Leith has been transformed; the old slums are now expensive bistros, and the red-light district has been pushed out of sight by urban regeneration.

Commercial Street is no longer a place of fear. It's a place of commerce and respectability. Despite all this, the memory of Sheila Anderson persists, like a stain under a fresh coat of paint.

Her murder remains one of Scotland's most notorious cold cases, not because of the mystery of who did it; it was likely a local man, a violent punter, but because of why he got away with it.

He got away with it because, for a few crucial days in April 1983, the system looked at Sheila Anderson and decided she didn't matter enough. There is no memorial at Gypsy Brae. The wind still whips off the Forth, cold and salt-laden.

Sheila's story is a reminder that the "Athens of the North" has a dark basement. It reminds us that while the tourists were looking at the Castle, women were dying in the Port.

The killer is likely old now, if not dead, having lived a life that he denied Sheila. He walked the streets of Edinburgh, perhaps passing the very spot where he picked her up, knowing that the city had forgiven him by forgetting him.

In the genre of Scottish Noir, there is usually a detective, a Rebus or a Taggart, who drinks too much but always gets the bad guy. Neat endings like that, emotionally satisfying as they are, generally belong in the realms of fiction.

In the true story of Sheila Anderson, the detectives went home, the case file was placed into a box, and the bad guy got away with it.

And that is the coldest reality of all.

THE GIRL IN THE CAVE (OR, THE LONG WAIT AT BRANDY COVE)

Wales, 1919

The Gower Peninsula is a place of savage beauty.

It sits on the south coast of Wales, a jagged finger of limestone jutting out into the Bristol Channel. In summer, it is a paradise of golden sands and surfers. But in the winter of 1919, it was a desolate, wind-scoured edge of the world. The cliffs were grey, the sea was violent, and the isolation was absolute.

It was here, in a lonely cottage overlooking the waves, that a twenty-six-year-old woman named Mamie Stuart disappeared. She didn't run away. She didn't take a train to London. She didn't leave a note. She simply ceased to exist.

For forty years, her fate was the great unsolved riddle of Welsh crime. Everyone knew she was dead. Everyone knew who killed her. But without a body, without evidence, the law was helpless. The man responsible walked free, lived a full life, and died in his bed.

It was only when three boys went exploring in a cave, decades too late, that the earth finally gave up its secret.

Mamie Stuart was not built for the quiet life. She was a chorus girl from Sunderland, vibrant, pretty, and thoroughly modern. She liked clothes, she liked attention, and she liked the bright lights. In 1918, she met George Shotton.

Shotton was a marine surveyor. He was older, heavyset, and projected an air of solid, middle-class respectability. To Mamie, he must have looked like security. He had money, he liked to travel, and he offered her a life far away from the stage door.

They married, or at least, Mamie thought they married. In 1919, they moved to the Gower where they rented a cottage called Ty Llangwm near Caswell Bay. It was picturesque, but it was also incredibly lonely. For a girl used to the hustle and bustle of the theatre, the silence of the cliffs must have been deafening. And it soon became clear that the silence wasn't peaceful; it was suffocating.

The marriage was a lie in more ways than one. George Shotton was a bigamist. He already had a wife and child living in Penarth, just up the coast. He was juggling two lives, playing the dutiful husband in one town and the doting partner in another.

But at Ty Llangwm, the mask was slipping. The "doting" partner was becoming a jailer. Neighbours, what few there were, noticed the change. Mamie, once so lively and full of life, had become withdrawn. There were arguments. Shouting matches that drifted over the garden walls. Shotton was jealous, controlling, and increasingly volatile.

And then, Christmas 1919 arrived. Mamie sent a telegram to her parents in Sunderland wishing them a happy holiday. It was the last time anyone ever heard from her. When Mamie stopped writing, her parents became worried, so they contacted the police.

In early 1920, investigators arrived at the cottage. Shotton was cool, calm, and collected. He told them the oldest story in the book: "She left me."

He claimed they had argued, that she had packed a bag, walked out the door, and returned to her old life. She was a chorus girl, after all. Flighty. Unreliable. It was a plausible lie, tailored to the prejudices of the time, one likely accepted by most police forces at the time.

To their credit, the police in Wales weren't buying it, so they searched the cottage. They found Mamie's clothes. All of them. Her coats, her dresses, her shoes. Why would a woman who loved fashion leave her entire wardrobe behind? Shotton went quiet.

Then they found the trunk. It was a heavy leather travel trunk, but the strap had been cut. Inside, there were strange stains, and the police were certain they were blood. The police were convinced they were looking at a murder scene. However, in 1920 a stain was legally just a stain. Forensics hadn't yet developed a way of detecting blood and proving what a stain was.

That didn't stop the police. They brought in sniffer dogs to scour the cliffs. They dredged the local wells. They searched the dunes. The press descended, sensing a scandal. The headlines wrote themselves: The Bigamist and the Missing Beauty.

Despite all this effort, sadly, they found nothing.

In 1920, the legal principle of corpus delicti, "the body of the crime," was a formidable barrier. Without a body, it was almost impossible to prove a murder had taken place. Legally, you couldn't just assume she was dead. She might be in America. She might be in hiding.

The police, though, knew. In an era where countless women were failed by the system, the Wales police did as much as they could to find the evidence needed, and when the evidence couldn't be found? They decided to go after Shotton a different way. They charged him with bigamy, as it was the only thing they could make stick. He was convicted and sentenced to eighteen months of hard labour. It was a slap on the wrist, a placeholder punishment for a much darker crime, but to the police it was better than nothing.

When he was released, George Shotton walked away, and lived the rest of his life as a free man. Though he never felt free. The police were a constant in his life, watching him, hoping for him to make a mistake. In 1958, he died in a hospital in Bristol. He took his secret to the grave, likely believing he had won, that he had committed the perfect crime, though given how the police hounded him the victory must have felt hollow.

In November 1961, three years after Shotton died and over forty years after Mamie vanished, three young potholers were exploring the caves at Brandy Cove, not far from the old cottage.

Brandy Cove is a rugged inlet, popular with smugglers in centuries past. There was an old lead mine there, a dark, damp shaft that ran deep into the cliffside. The entrance had been blocked by a heavy stone slab for as long as anyone could remember.

Curiosity is a powerful force. The boys managed to move the slab. They squeezed into the darkness, their torches cutting through the gloom.

Inside, they found a sack. When they touched it, it crumbled, and out rolled a human skull.

The police were called. This time, the technology was better, but they didn't really need it, as the skeleton was wearing a wedding ring. A gold ring. Inside the band, the inscription was still legible: George to Mamie, 1918.

There was other jewellery, too, items that Mamie's

family had described in 1920. But the most chilling discovery was the state of the remains. The skeleton had been roughly sawn into three distinct pieces.

This hadn't been a crime of passion where a body was hidden in a panic. This was cold, industrial, disposal. Shotton had dismembered his wife, likely in the cottage, and then carried her, piece by piece, to the abandoned mine shaft. He had hidden her behind a slab of rock that he knew would be too heavy for casual passers-by to move. He had buried her in a stone safe, just a few hundred yards from where they had lived.

The coroner's inquest in 1961 was a surreal affair. It was, in essence, the trial of a ghost.

The verdict was "Unlawful Killing." The cause of death couldn't be definitively determined after four decades, but the sawing of the bones told its own story. The police confirmed what everyone already knew: George Shotton was the killer.

If Mamie had been found just a few years earlier, Shotton would have been an old man in the dock, facing a life sentence. Instead, he had cheated justice. He had lived a full span of years while Mamie lay in the dark, waiting for someone to move the stone, which is why this story feels at home in a book of unsolved cases.

There is a final, cruel, twist to the story.

After the inquest, Mamie's remains were not immediately returned to her family. In a bizarre administrative decision, the Cardiff University anatomy department kept the skeleton. For decades, Mamie Stuart, the vibrant chorus girl who loved to dance, gathered dust in a cupboard, labelled as a specimen.

It wasn't until 2019, a full century after she disappeared, that she was finally laid to rest. Her great-niece arranged for her to be buried in the family plot in Sunderland.

She finally went home.

THE JUDGE'S DAUGHTER (OR, MURDER AT THE GLEN)

Belfast, 1952
In 1952, Northern Ireland was a place where everybody knew their place. It was a society stacked like a wedding cake. At the bottom, the workers in the shipyards and the linen mills. In the middle, the shopkeepers and the clerks. And at the very top, untouchable and remote, lived the legal establishment.

They lived in big houses behind high walls. They dined at the Reform Club. They administered the law, but they did not necessarily feel bound by the same rules as the people they judged, and nowhere was this divide more apparent than at The Glen.

The Glen was a sprawling Victorian mansion in Whiteabbey, a wealthy enclave just north of Belfast. It was surrounded by dense trees and long, sweeping, lawns. It was the home of the Curran family.

The head of the household was Lancelot Curran, a High Court Judge and the former Attorney General. He was a man of immense power and a pillar of the Unionist establishment. To cross him was considered to be professional suicide. To suspect his family of a crime was unthinkable.

But on the night of November 12, 1952, the unthinkable arrived on his doorstep. His nineteen-year-old daughter, Patricia, was found dead in the driveway. She had been stabbed thirty-seven times.

What followed was not a murder investigation. It was a masterclass in how the establishment protects its own. It was a story of a frantic tidying up, a scapegoat plucked from the margins, and a silence that has hung over Belfast legal circles for over seventy years.

Patricia Curran was a student at Queen's University. By the standards of 1950s Belfast, she was considered "wild," which simply meant she had opinions, a social life, and didn't fit neatly into the box of a debutante. She was lively, intelligent, and perhaps a little unhappy at home.

On that November evening, she took the bus home from the university, getting off at Whiteabbey around 5:00 p.m. The walk from the bus stop to the gates of The Glen was short. The driveway itself was a quarter of a mile long, winding through the trees. It was dark, wet, and silent.

Patricia started walking up that drive. She never made it to the front door.

When Patricia didn't appear for dinner, the family grew concerned, or so the story goes. At around 1:45 a.m., hours after she should have arrived, her father, Judge Curran, and her brother, Desmond, a barrister described as a deeply religious man, went out to look for her.

They found her body lying in the shrubbery, just twenty yards from the house. The scene they described was horrific. Patricia had been stabbed repeatedly in the face and neck. It was a frenzied attack, an explosion of rage.

But almost immediately, the facts blurred, and the real questions began.

When the police arrived, led by RUC Inspector Albert McConnell, they found a scene that defied the laws of physics. Patricia had been stabbed thirty-seven times, yet there was almost no blood on the ground where she lay.

Her books and papers were neatly stacked nearby. Her clothes were dry, despite the fact that it had been raining heavily all evening.

Any detective worth his badge would have looked at that scene and drawn one conclusion: that wasn't where she was killed. Logic and physics showed she must have been killed somewhere indoors, somewhere dry, and then dragged outside and dumped in the bushes after the rain had stopped.

And there was only one building nearby: The Glen.

In any ordinary murder case, the first rule is to suspect the family and the second rule is to seal the crime scene. Neither of these things happened.

Inspector McConnell found himself in an impossible position. He was a policeman; Lancelot Curran was a High Court Judge. In the hierarchy of Northern Ireland at the time, the Judge was God. You didn't interrogate God. You didn't fingerprint God's wife or son. And you certainly didn't tear up God's floorboards looking for bloodstains.

The house was never treated as a crime scene. The family was treated with deference and sympathy. Lady Doris Curran, Patricia's mother, was sedated and kept away from questioning. Desmond, the brother, was allowed to control the narrative.

The police accepted the family's timeline without any challenge. They accepted the idea that a maniac had been lurking in the bushes in the pouring rain, waiting for a specific girl, had killed her in a frenzy, without leaving a pool of blood behind, and then vanished into the night. All whilst somehow managing to keep the girls clothes and possessions dry during a torrential rain storm.

They accepted that, when it came to The Glen, the laws of physics simply didn't apply.

The focus of the investigation was immediately, and aggressively, directed outwards. They needed a stranger to point the figure at and they found one in Iain Hay Gordon.

Iain Hay Gordon was twenty years old. He was a Scottish conscript doing his National Service with the RAF at Edenmore, a base not far from Whiteabbey. He was the perfect suspect for a frame-up. He was an outsider, being Scottish, and he was socially awkward. He had no powerful family to protect him. And, crucially, he had a "weak personality."

The police brought him in. They grilled him for three days without a solicitor. They played on his anxieties. They suggested that perhaps he had blacked out. Perhaps he had done it and forgotten. Finally, exhausted due to sleep deprivation, and terrified after several savage beatings that had left him with broken ribs, Gordon signed a confession.

It was a confession riddled with errors. It got basic details of the crime wrong. It described a weapon that was never found and, even if it was, couldn't have been used in the murder. Hammers aren't renowned for their ability to inflict knife wounds. None of that mattered.

The trial was a farce, even by the standards of the day.

The defence, led by a QC who was a close personal friend of the Curran family, didn't even try to prove Gordon's innocence. Instead, he pushed for a verdict of "Guilty, but Insane."

Why? Because a "Not Guilty" verdict would mean the police would have to go back to The Glen and start asking the Judge awkward questions about him and his family. A simple "Guilty" verdict would lead to a hanging, and hanging a twenty-year-old boy on flimsy evidence was likely to provoke a public outcry and an appeal, and this was a case that they didn't want placed under scrutiny.

"Guilty, but Insane" was a compromise likely reached behind closed doors. It meant Gordon wouldn't hang, but he would be locked up indefinitely in a mental asylum. The case would be closed. The file would be sealed. The Judge's reputation would remain spotless and his powerful family could continue to live their lives.

It worked. In March 1953, Iain Hay Gordon was sent

to Holywell Hospital. He would spend seven years there, before being quietly released, and sent back to Scotland. He was legally still a convicted murderer, but at the age of 28, he was once again a free man.

He spent nearly half a century fighting to clear his name. In 2000, the case was finally referred to the Court of Appeal. The judges looked at the evidence, the coerced confession given after what amounted to torture, the dry clothes, the impossible timeline, and quashed the conviction.

Finally, Gordon was proven to be innocent, but his victory was hollow. The constant delays of the appeal, making Gordon wait until the year 2000, looks like a deliberate act to hide the truth.

By then Lancelot Curran was dead, Doris was dead, and Desmond was dead. The house was gone. There was no one left to answer the questions needed to bring Patricia's killer to justice.

The police file, when it was finally examined, revealed the depths of the cover-up. Footprints at the scene had been ignored. Witness statements that contradicted the family's account had been intentionally suppressed. It was a conspiracy of silence, orchestrated by men who believed that the reputation of the judiciary was worth more than the life of a Scottish airman.

For decades, Belfast whispered about what really happened that night, and what evidence the demolition hid. The theories all pointed inwards.

The second the trial ended, the Curran

family abandoned The Glen. They moved out almost immediately, demolishing the building, thus destroying any evidence that might point to what actually happened to Patricia. To the people of Belfast, who were used to the British establishment covering up after their own, it was as if they couldn't get away from the walls fast enough.

The "dry clothes" and the lack of blood suggest Patricia was killed inside the house. The frenzied nature of the stabbing, thirty-seven wounds, mostly to the face, suggest a personal, emotional attack, rather than a sexual assault by a stranger.

Was it the mother? Lady Doris Curran was known to be fragile and reportedly had a volatile relationship with her daughter. Did an argument spiral out of control?

Was it the brother? Desmond Curran was a complex figure, intensely religious, and reportedly repressed. Did he snap?

Or was it the Judge himself? We can't say for sure but we can put forward a theory. A theory very different to the case against Gordon. This is a theory that the known evidence supports.

Patricia was killed in the hallway or the study of The Glen. The family, terrified of the scandal, spent the hours between her death, and the "discovery," cleaning up the crime scene. They waited for the rain to stop before carrying her body out to the driveway.

Once the scene was staged, the Judge called the police, relying on the absolute certainty that no constable would dare question his word, let alone accuse him of murder. In Northern Ireland at the time? He WAS the law.

The murder of Patricia Curran is more than just a whodunnit. It is a portrait of a society where power was absolute. It is a story about the "Big House" mentality. The idea that what happens behind the gates of the gentry stays behind the gates.

If you go to Whiteabbey today, The Glen is long gone. Modern housing estates cover the land where the long driveway once wound through the trees. The physical traces of the crime have been erased by suburbia but the story remains a stain on the history of Northern Ireland.

We would like to think that, in the present day, what happened to Patricia couldn't happen again. We want to believe that the law applies equally to everyone, and that the rich and powerful can no longer escape justice simply by the nature of their position.

A glance at recent headlines, however, suggests we are still living in a time where cover-ups are the norm. A time where powerful men can commit horrific crimes, knowing full well that they have the money and influence to bury the truth, and that justice is something they are unlikely to ever face.

They have the power to play the courts today, rigging the system to ensure the results they want—in exactly the same way Lancelot Curran did back in 1952.

Some things, unfortunately, never change.

THE BLACK DAHLIA

Part I: The Mannequin in the Weeds

On the morning of January 15, 1947, Los Angeles was waking up to a day that felt like a postcard. The sky was a sharp, unblemished blue. The air was cool but promised the kind of dry warmth that drew thousands of people to the West Coast every month. The war was over. The servicemen were home. The aircraft factories were humming, and Hollywood was churning out dreams at a steady twenty-four frames per second.

Los Angeles was the city of the future. It was a sprawling grid of optimism, new housing developments, and freshly paved roads stretching out into the desert.

One of those developments was Leimert Park. It was a respectable neighbourhood, a place for the middle class to trim their lawns and park their cars. But on the edge of the district, on the west side of South Norton Avenue, there was an undeveloped patch of land. It was a vacant lot, overgrown with tall weeds and scrub grass, a gap in the smile of the city.

At around 10:00 a.m., a housewife named Betty Bersinger was walking south on Norton Avenue. She was heading to a shoe repair shop, pushing her three-year-old daughter, Anne, in a pushchair.

As she passed the vacant lot, her eyes were drawn to something lying in the grass a few feet from the sidewalk.

At first glance, her brain refused to categorize it as human. The object was too white. It was too broken. It looked, she later told the police, like a mannequin —perhaps a piece of debris discarded by a department store window dresser, broken in half and tossed into the weeds.

Betty stopped. She looked closer. And the illusion of the mannequin shattered. She realized with a jolt of nausea that she was looking at human skin. She grabbed the handle of the stroller, turned her body to block her daughter's view, and ran to the nearest house to call the police.

She had just found the body of Elizabeth Short. And in doing so, she had opened the door to a nightmare that Los Angeles would never wake up from.

When the first patrol officers, Frank Perkins and Will Fitzgerald, arrived at the scene, they found a tableau so grotesque that it seemed staged for an audience. This was not a chaotic crime scene. There was no struggle in the dirt. There was no blood spatter on the grass. The body had been placed there with chilling precision.

The victim was a young woman with jet-black hair and pale skin. She was naked. And she had been cut completely in half at the waist.

The bisection was not a jagged tear; it was a clean, methodical separation. The two halves of her torso lay a few inches apart. Her lower half was positioned straight, but her upper torso was turned slightly. Her arms were raised above her head, bent at the elbows in a posture of surrender or perhaps exhibition.

But it was the lack of blood that unnerved the officers most.

A human body contains roughly ten pints of blood. To cut a person in half is a catastrophic, messy event. Yet the body of Elizabeth Short was drained. She was marble-white, completely exsanguinated. There was no blood on the ground beneath her, save for a few negligible drops, and no blood on the body itself. She had been scrubbed clean.

This detail alone told the police something vital within the first five minutes: The vacant lot on Norton Avenue was not a murder scene; it was a dumping ground. It was a gallery. The killer had murdered her elsewhere—in a place with running water, drainage, and privacy—and then transported the two halves of her body to this public spot, reassembling her like a broken doll for the morning commuters to find.

As the detectives from the LAPD Homicide Division arrived—legendary figures like Harry Hansen and Finis Brown—they began to catalogue the injuries. The list was a litany of sadism that suggested a killer who hated women with a biblical intensity.

The body bore the marks of prolonged torture. There were rope burns on her wrists and ankles, indicating she had been bound for hours, perhaps days. There were bruises and lacerations on her breasts. There were chunks of flesh gouged out.

But the most defining injury—the one that would haunt the public imagination for nearly a century—was on her face.

The killer had taken a knife and carved a deep gash from the corners of her mouth toward her ears. It was a "Glasgow Smile," a grotesque, permanent grin that turned her face into a mask of mockery.

It was an injury designed to dehumanize. It stripped

her of her expression, her beauty, and her ability to be viewed as a person. In death, she was forced to smile at the horror of her own destruction.

Further examination revealed even darker details. The body had been posed carefully. The intestines had been tucked neatly under the buttocks of the lower torso. The separation of the spine had been done between the second and third lumbar vertebrae—a precise cut that avoided bone, slipping the knife through the soft cartilage.

This wasn't a frenzy. This was work.

By noon, the vacant lot on Norton Avenue had transformed into a circus.

In 1947, crime scene protocol was loose. There was no yellow tape, no forensic tents shielding the body from view. As news of the discovery spread—amplified by the arrival of press photographers with their bulky Speed Graphic cameras—the public began to arrive.

They stood on the sidewalk. They trampled the weeds. Men in fedoras and women in housecoats peered over the shoulders of the uniformed officers. Some reports say that reporters arrived before the coroner, trampling potential footprints and compromising evidence in their rush to get the "money shot."

The flashbulbs popped, illuminating the pale skin against the dark grass. The photos taken that morning would become some of the most famous and disturbing images in the history of photography. They captured the surreal contrast of the scene: the bright California sun, the mundane suburban houses in the background, and the broken, mutilated form in the foreground.

It was the ultimate collision of the American Dream

and the American Nightmare.

As the body was finally removed—taken away in two separate pieces—the coroner, Dr. Frederick Newbarr, began his work. His autopsy report would deepen the mystery.

The cause of death was determined to be a cerebral haemorrhage caused by blows to the head, combined with shock from the lacerations to the face. She had been alive when the face was cut. She had been alive when the blows were struck.

But the bisection—the cutting in half—had occurred after death.

This detail sparked a debate that rages to this day: Was the killer a doctor?

The bisection was performed with a degree of skill that suggested anatomical knowledge. The killer knew exactly where to cut to separate the spine without sawing through bone. This procedure, known as a hemicorporectomy, is not something an average person could perform cleanly. It suggested a surgeon, a medical student, or perhaps a skilled butcher.

However, other experts argued that the cut was crude in places, suggesting someone mimicking skill rather than possessing it. But the "Doctor Theory" took root immediately. It fits the noir narrative perfectly: a mad surgeon operating in a hidden room, draining the blood, scrubbing the body, and then driving into the night to display his handiwork.

Why Norton Avenue? This question plagued the detectives. The location felt specific. It wasn't a hidden canyon or a deep ditch. It was a roadside lot in a developing neighbourhood. The body was placed just feet from the sidewalk. The killer wanted her to be found.

More than that, the killer wanted her to be seen. The posing of the body—the legs spread, the arms raised—was a taunt. It was a display of dominance. The killer was saying: Look what I can do. Look how I can take a human being and turn them into a thing.

The lack of blood and the washing of the body suggested a strange kind of intimacy, or perhaps a desire to erase the messiness of the murder while preserving the horror of the result. It was a contradiction: a savage mutilation presented as a clean, almost sterile exhibit.

As the sun set on January 15, 1947, the vacant lot was finally empty. But the image of what had lain there was burned into the retinas of everyone who saw it.

The police had a body. They had a crime scene that offered no clues—no footprints, no tire tracks, no weapon.

And they had a victim who, at that moment, was just "Jane Doe Number 1."

They didn't yet know her name was Elizabeth Short. They didn't know she would become the Black Dahlia.

All they knew was that something evil had walked the streets of Los Angeles, and for the first time in a long time, the City of Angels felt like it had been abandoned by God.

Part II: The Ink and the Blood

If the discovery of the body was a tragedy, what followed was a feeding frenzy.

In 1947, Los Angeles was a company town, and the company was the media. Aggressive, brawling newspapers—the Los Angeles Examiner, the Herald-Express, the Times dominated the city. They fought for circulation with the same ferocity that gangsters fought for turf.

When the call came in about the body on Norton Avenue, the editors smelled blood. But a body is just a body until it has a name. Without an identity, the victim was just another dead girl in a city full of them. To sell papers, they needed a story. They needed a life to deconstruct.

The race to identify Jane Doe Number 1 wasn't won by the police. It was won by the press. The Soundphoto Miracle

The Los Angeles Examiner, owned by the formidable William Randolph Hearst, had an ace up its sleeve: technology.

The police had taken fingerprints from the corpse. In a standard investigation, these prints would be mailed to the FBI in Washington, D.C., a process that took days. But the Examiner offered the LAPD a deal with the devil. They possessed a Soundphoto machine—a precursor to the fax machine—that could transmit images over telephone lines.

They told the detectives: Let us scan the prints and send them to Washington. We'll get you an ID in hours, not days. All we ask in return is the exclusive. The police, desperate for a lead, agreed.

The prints were beamed across the country. In Washington, the FBI matched them almost instantly. The victim's prints were on file for two reasons: she had applied for a job at an Army base in 1943, and she had been arrested in Santa Barbara for underage drinking later that same year.

The teletype chattered back a name: Elizabeth Short. She was twenty-two years old. She was from Medford, Massachusetts. She had come to Hollywood, like thousands of others, chasing a vague dream of fame that had ended in a vacant lot.

The police had their name. But the Examiner had the scoop. And they were about to demonstrate exactly how ruthless they could be.

What the Examiner did next remains one of the darkest chapters in the history of journalism.

Before the police could notify the next of kin, reporters tracked down Elizabeth's mother, Phoebe Short, in Medford. They got her on the phone. But rather than tell her that her daughter had been murdered, they told Phoebe that Elizabeth had won a beauty contest. They played on a mother's pride. They pumped her for information, asking about Elizabeth's life, her friends, her habits, her history. Phoebe, delighted, chatted away, giving them the background colour they needed for their front page.

Only after they had wrung every drop of information out of her did they drop the hammer.

"Actually, Mrs. Short, your daughter didn't win a contest. She's dead. Her body was found in a vacant lot in Los Angeles. She's been sliced in two."

They weren't done yet. Some accounts say they even offered to pay for Phoebe's flight to LA, not out of kindness, but to ensure she would speak only to them when she arrived. It was a masterclass in exploitation. The press had turned a grieving mother into a source, and then a headline.

With a name in hand, the newspapers went to work

building a myth.

"Elizabeth Short" was too plain. It sounded like a schoolteacher or a librarian. To sell the horror of the crime, they needed something more exotic. They needed a label that hinted at sex, mystery, and danger.

They found it in a nickname she had reportedly been given by customers at a drug store in Long Beach: The Black Dahlia.

It was a riff on the popular 1946 movie The Blue Dahlia, a film noir about a murdered wife. It fit Elizabeth perfectly. She had jet-black hair. She preferred black clothing. She was striking, pale, and enigmatic.

The press seized on it. Overnight, Elizabeth Short ceased to be a human being. She became The Black Dahlia. The name did two things. First, it glamorised her death. It turned a gritty, sordid murder into a dark fairy tale. Second, it dehumanized her. A "Dahlia" is a thing, an object, a character. It is easier to read about the mutilation of a "Dahlia" than the torture of a twenty-two-year-old girl who liked to write letters to her mother.

The relationship between the LAPD and the press wasn't just close; it was incestuous.

Reporters swarmed the Homicide Division. They sat on desks. They listened in on calls. In the chaos of the first few days, reporters from the Herald-Express were literally answering the phones in the police station, taking tips from the public before the detectives even heard them.

If a tip sounded good, the reporters would rush to the scene, interview the witness, and trample the evidence before the police cruiser even pulled up. They withheld information. They hid witnesses in hotel rooms to keep them exclusive. They spun theories that had no basis in fact.

One day, the headlines screamed that the Dahlia was a "man-crazy delinquent." The next, she was a "tortured innocent." They painted her as a prostitute (there was no evidence she ever traded sex for money), a lesbian, a drifter, a tease. They projected the city's anxieties onto her corpse.

The investigation was drowning in ink. The police couldn't tell which leads were real and which were generated by the morning edition.

And then, the killer joined the conversation.

On January 21, nine days after the body was found, the Examiner received a package. It had been mailed from a drop box near the Biltmore Hotel—one of the last places Elizabeth was seen alive.

The envelope was addressed in letters cut from newspaper headlines and pasted together, a classic ransom-note style that felt almost theatrical. It read:

"Here is Dahlia's belongings letter to follow."

Inside the envelope were Elizabeth Short's birth certificate, her social security card, photos, and an address book. The items had been wiped clean with gasoline, erasing any fingerprints. The smell of the fuel was still pungent when the editor opened the packet.

This was a taunt. The killer was reading the papers. He saw the circus, and he wanted to be the ringmaster. By sending the items to the press, not the police, he proved that he understood the game. He knew that the newspaper would splash the proof on the front page, feeding his ego.

The address book was the Holy Grail. It contained the

names of seventy-five men.

The police launched a massive dragnet. They interviewed every man in the book. It was a parade of casual dates, old flames, and strangers who had bought her a drink. But it led nowhere. Most of the men barely knew her. Elizabeth was a girl who collected people, but rarely let them close.

The taunts didn't stop. A few days later, another letter arrived. This one was handwritten. It said:

"I will give up on Wed Jan 29, 10 am. Had my fun at police. Black Dahlia Avenger."

The police staked out the designated location. They waited. The press waited. The city held its breath. No one showed up.

Instead, another note arrived:

"Have changed my mind. You would not give me a square deal. Dahlia killing was justified."

The killer, if indeed these notes were from the killer and not a crank, was toying with them. He was enjoying the panic. He was shaping the narrative, framing the murder not as a crime of passion, but as a "justified" act, a moral correction.

As the weeks dragged on, the investigation began to fracture. The sheer volume of noise created by the press made it impossible to see the truth. The police were chasing thousands of leads. They checked out medical students (because of the bisection). They checked out butchers. They checked out sex offenders.

They raided the homes of doctors who had been struck off the register. They dragged the storm drains. They interviewed every bartender in Hollywood who claimed to have poured Elizabeth a drink.

But the media had muddied the water so thoroughly that the timeline of Elizabeth's last days became a blur. Had she been seen in San Diego? Or Chicago? Or the infamous Cecil Hotel? Every headline created a new false memory in the public consciousness.

The Examiner and the Herald had sold millions of papers. They had created a legend. But in doing so, they had helped the killer disappear. By turning the investigation into a spectacle, they had allowed the one person who knew the truth to slip away into the shadows, hidden behind a wall of newsprint.

The Black Dahlia was now the most famous woman in Los Angeles. But the man who made her that way was already becoming a ghost.

Part III: The Parade of the Damned

In the weeks following the discovery on Norton Avenue, the Los Angeles Police Department didn't have a shortage of suspects. They had a surplus. A high-profile murder often triggers a psychological phenomenon known as "confession fever," but the Black Dahlia case created an epidemic. It seemed that half the men in Los Angeles wanted to claim credit for the atrocity.

In the first few weeks, over fifty people confessed to the murder.

They walked into police stations. They called newspapers. They sent letters. They were a motley collection of the disturbed, the lonely, and the desperate. There were soldiers suffering from PTSD who believed they might have done it during a blackout. There were housewives who claimed they killed Elizabeth in a jealous rage. There were alcoholics who woke up with a hangover and a vague sense of guilt.

And then there was the man who walked into the station and confessed simply because he couldn't stand another night with his wife and her cooking.

He told the desk sergeant he had killed the Black Dahlia. When the detectives grilled him, his story fell apart immediately. He didn't know the details. He didn't know the location. He finally broke down and admitted the truth: he figured a few days in a holding cell was preferable to going home to his nagging spouse. He was charged with filing a false report, but he had already become a punchline in a tragedy.

This "Confession Brigade" clogged the gears of the investigation. Every time a new confessor appeared, detectives had to waste precious hours debunking their story, checking their alibis, and filing the paperwork. It was a smoke screen of human misery that allowed the real killer to stay hidden.

But amidst the noise, there were names that stuck. There were men who didn't confess, but who fit the profile so perfectly that they remain suspects to this day.

The first man in the cross-hairs was Robert "Red" Manley. Manley was a twenty-five-year-old hardware salesman with red hair and a wife at home. He was the quintessential "nice guy" who made a bad decision. He had picked Elizabeth up in San Diego. She needed a ride to Los Angeles; he offered her one.

They spent a chaste night in a motel (Elizabeth slept in her clothes; Manley slept in his). On January 9, he drove her to the Biltmore Hotel in down-town LA. She told him she was meeting her sister. He watched her walk into the lobby.

He was the last person confirmed to have seen her alive.

For the LAPD, Manley was the low-hanging fruit. He was the last link in the chain. They brought him in. They grilled him. They pumped him full of "truth serum" (sodium pentothal). They gave him multiple polygraph tests.

Manley passed everything. His story never wavered. He was a salesman who had helped a pretty girl and got nothing but ruin in return. The police eventually cleared him, but the press destroyed him. His marriage suffered. His mental health collapsed. He spent his later years in a mental institution, haunted by the drive to Los Angeles.

Red Manley was innocent of murder, but he was a casualty of the case nonetheless.

If Manley was the innocent dupe, Mark Hansen was the dark prince of the Hollywood underworld. Hansen was a wealthy, shadowy figure who owned the Florentine Gardens nightclub. He lived in a bungalow behind the club, a place that functioned as a crash pad for aspiring actresses and showgirls. Elizabeth Short had stayed there briefly in late 1946.

Hansen was infatuated with her. But Elizabeth, according to witnesses, had rejected his advances.

He became a prime suspect for several reasons. First, the address book mailed to the Examiner belonged to him—it was Mark Hansen's book, embossed with his name (though he claimed he had given it to Elizabeth). Second, he had a motive: rejection. Third, he had the means: a large house, privacy, and connections to the dark side of Hollywood.

But like Manley, the evidence wasn't quite there. Hansen had alibis. He had lawyers. He slipped through the net, leaving only a lingering suspicion that he knew more than he was saying.

Then there was Leslie Dillon. Dillon was an aspiring writer who worked as a bellhop. He contacted the LAPD psychiatrist, Dr. Paul De River, offering "theories" about the murder. He claimed he was writing a book about sadism.

Dillon knew things. He knew details about the crime scene that hadn't been released to the public. He spoke about a "friend" named Jeff Connors who he claimed was the killer.

The police began to suspect that "Jeff Connors" was imaginary, and that Dillon was confessing by proxy. They tracked him down. They held him in a hotel room in Las Vegas (illegally) and interrogated him.

It turned out "Jeff Connors" was real—a man named Artie Lane who worked as a maintenance man at the Columbia Studios lot. But the investigation into Dillon was botched so badly by the rogue psychiatrist that the LAPD had to back off to avoid a scandal. Dillon sued the department and won.

Was he the killer? Or just a man with a dark imagination who got too close to the fire?

But of all the suspects, one casts the longest shadow: Dr. George Hodel. Hodel was a genius, a prodigy, and a monster. He was a physician with a high IQ and a taste for the avant-garde. He lived in the Sowden House, a distinctive, temple-like mansion in Hollywood that looked like a fortress.

Hodel ran a clinic for venereal diseases. He knew

anatomy. He had the surgical skills to perform the bisection (he had actually been trained in that specific procedure). Rumours swirled that Hodel held orgies at the Sowden House, parties fuelled by drugs and sadism. His own daughter accused him of incest.

The LAPD took Hodel seriously. In 1950, they planted microphones in his home. For weeks, they listened to the doctor's life. They heard him arguing. They heard sounds of assaults. And on one chilling tape, they heard him say:

"Supposin' I did kill the Black Dahlia. They couldn't prove it now. They can't talk to my secretary because she's dead."

It sounded like a confession. It sounded like the smoking gun. But Hodel had friends in high places. He moved in circles of power. Just as the heat was getting too intense, he packed his bags and moved to the Philippines. He lived there for decades, untouchable. It's an all too familiar story.

Years later, his own son, Steve Hodel, a respected former LAPD homicide detective. would write best-selling books laying out the case against his father. He argued that the Sowden House was the murder site, that Hodel was a serial killer responsible for the Dahlia and other "Lone Woman" murders.

The Hodel theory is compelling. It fits the "Doctor" profile. It explains the surgical skill. It explains the arrogance. But George Hodel died a free man. The wiretaps were buried in the vaults. The Sowden House kept its secrets.

The tragedy of the investigation was that the LAPD had too many pieces and no picture.

They had a surgeon (Hodel). They had a gangster

(Hansen). They had a drifter (Dillon). They had hundreds of false confessors.

Every time they focused on one, the evidence for another would pop up. The "Doctor" theory explained the cut, but not the motive. The "Gangster" theory explained the motive, but not the cut.

And lurking behind it all was the corruption of 1947 Los Angeles. This was a city where police officers could be bought, where evidence could disappear, and where the reputation of the department was often more important than justice.

By the early 1950s, the Homicide Division had thousands of index cards, hundreds of interviews, and a room full of physical evidence. But the momentum was gone. The detectives who worked the case originally began to retire or die.

The Black Dahlia case didn't end with a bang. It ended with a slow, agonizing fade. The file remains open. But the men who might have done it—the men who hated women enough to carve a smile into a face—are all gone.

They left behind a city that would never be innocent again, and a list of suspects that reads like a casting call for a nightmare.

Part IV: The Flower and the Ghost

Seventy years later, we know everything about the Black Dahlia.

We know the geometry of her injuries. We know the contents of her stomach, faecal matter, suggesting another indignity. We know the names of the men she dated and the motels she slept in. We know the conspiracy theories, the noir legends, and the lurid headlines.

But we know almost nothing about Elizabeth Short.

Somewhere along the way, between the coroner's slab and the movie screen, the woman herself was erased. She became a prop in her own tragedy. She became a cautionary tale, a Halloween costume, a "case."

To solve the Black Dahlia, or at least, to understand it, we have to stop looking at the body in the weeds and start looking at the girl who lived.

Elizabeth Short was not a "vamp." She wasn't a prostitute. She wasn't a creature of the night.

She was a middle child from Massachusetts, born into a family that cracked down the middle during the Great Depression. Her father, Cleo Short, built miniature golf courses until the stock market crashed, after which he faked his own suicide and vanished, leaving his wife Phoebe to raise five daughters alone.

Elizabeth grew up in a house defined by absence. She had asthma. She loved movies. She spent her teenage years dreaming of a life that was bigger, brighter, and less grey than Medford.

When she was nineteen, her father reappeared in California. Elizabeth got on a train to Vallejo to live with him. It was a disaster. Cleo expected a housekeeper; Elizabeth wanted a father. They argued. She left. This was the beginning of her drifting. She worked in the exchange at Camp Cooke. She was voted "Camp Cutie." She fell in love with a pilot named Major Matthew Gordon Jr. He was the love of her life. They wrote letters. They planned a future.

But this was 1945. The telegram came just days before the Japanese surrender. Matt Gordon had crashed in

India. He was dead.

Elizabeth Short didn't die on Norton Avenue in 1947. A part of her died in 1945, when she opened that telegram, taking away her planned future.

The Elizabeth Short who arrived in Los Angeles in 1946 was a ghost in waiting. She was grieving. She was unmoored. She didn't have an apartment. She lived out of a suitcase, moving from hotels to rooming houses to the sofas of friends. She was one of thousands of young women in post-war LA who existed on the margins of the Hollywood dream.

The press painted her as "man-crazy," but the reality was more mundane and more heartbreaking. She dated men for dinner. She dated men for company. She dated men because she couldn't afford to buy a steak on her own.

She was a "teaser," the men complained. She would go to dinner, go to the club, but she wouldn't go to bed.

This wasn't malice; it was survival. And perhaps it was grief. She was still wearing Matt Gordon's engagement ring in her heart, if not on her finger. She was protecting herself in a city that viewed women as currency.

She wasn't a femme fatale. She was just lonely.

The murder killed Elizabeth Short, but the investigation obliterated her. The nickname, The Black Dahlia, was the first act of vandalism. It turned her into a character. It allowed the public to read about the "Dahlia's" mutilation without feeling the pain of a human being.

Then came the slut-shaming. The police and the press needed a reason why this had happened. It was too terrifying to believe that a nice girl could be snatched and butchered for no reason. So, they invented a reason. She asked for it. She hung around with the wrong crowd. She teased the wrong man.

They stripped her of her dignity. They published her autopsy photos. They printed the names in her address book. They turned her life into a dirty joke.

Even today, you can buy t-shirts with her severed face on them. You can take "Black Dahlia" tours in Los Angeles that stop at the places she was miserable. We have turned her agony into entertainment. In doing so, we have completed the killer's work. He wanted to dehumanize her. By treating her as a puzzle rather than a person, we are complicit in that dehumanisation.

The Black Dahlia case is the ultimate trap for the armchair detective. It invites us in. It offers us clues that seem to fit together perfectly, until they don't. It was the Doctor! It was the Mobster! It was the Bellhop!

We sit in our homes, eighty years later, and we move the pieces around. We feel a thrill when we think we've spotted a connection the LAPD missed. We write books. We make podcasts. We solve the crime over and over again. But there is a danger in this.

When we play detective with a case like this, we risk forgetting the reality of the violence. We treat the bisection as a "clue" rather than an atrocity. We treat the "Glasgow Smile" as a signature rather than a scream.

The Black Dahlia case isn't a game of Cluedo. It isn't a Sherlock Holmes story where the loose ends are tied up in the final chapter. It's not an episode of Midsomer Murders or Murder, She Wrote.

It is a story about a young woman who was tortured to

death. It is a story about a system that failed to protect her and then failed to avenge her.

So, how do we tell this story responsibly?

We start by giving her back her name.

Elizabeth Short.

She liked Deanna Durbin movies. She didn't drink much because it made her sick. She had a laugh that people remembered. She wrote to her mother every week. She wore a black coat because she thought it made her look sophisticated, like the women in the magazines.

She was twenty-two years old. She had her whole life ahead of her.

She walked out of the Biltmore Hotel on January 9, 1947, and walked into the darkness. She was scared. She was alone. The mystery of who killed her is seductive. It draws us in with its shadows and its secrets. But the greater mystery, and the greater tragedy, is the loss of the woman she might have become.

Maybe she would have gone back to Medford. Maybe she would have met someone else. Maybe she would have found a job she loved. Maybe she would have grown old, had children, and died in a warm bed surrounded by family.

That future was stolen and no amount of sleuthing, no amount of books, and no amount of "case closed" declarations can ever give it back.

The case of the Black Dahlia remains unsolved. And perhaps that is fitting. Because as long as it remains open, we are forced to keep looking at her. We are forced to keep saying her name.

We cannot save her. But we can remember her. Not as the mannequin in the weeds. Not as the Dahlia. But as Elizabeth.

The girl who just wanted to be seen, and who ended up being watched by the whole world, forever.

AFTERWORD

I want to thank you for reading this book, and for walking through these dark streets with me. Before we part ways, I would like to end with one last personal story.

In 2017, I was still relying on a walking stick following my cancer surgery in 2003. I had tried to be rid of it, with limited success. My recovery was slow, painful, and admittedly hampered by my own lack of patience.

Then I saw an advert for, of all things, a men's cabaret dance class. At the time, I was going through a journey of finding myself, deciding who I wanted to be in this world. For some reason, the idea appealed to me.

Over the course of several months, I learned the steps to a Charleston and a routine to ZZ Top, all while rebuilding the strength in my leg. Lara, the dance teacher, was also a physiotherapist. She was the first person who framed the question not as "what can't you do," but rather "what can you do?"

It inspired me to keep pushing that recovery. As of this writing, it has been over seven years since I last used a stick.

The lessons were on the other side of the city, requiring a lengthy bus journey followed by a walk in the dark.

And then, in December 2017, the violence found me.

I was walking to my lesson when, before I could even process the movement, I was punched from behind. Somehow, I managed to stay on my feet while two lads confronted me, demanding my phone and my wallet "or else…"

You never know how you'll react in a situation like that until you are standing in the middle of it. We talk about "fight or flight." We ask ourselves: Do we run, or do we hold our ground.

I did neither.

I burst out laughing.

With blood pouring from my mouth, I found the entire situation absurd. In my head, time had slowed down. My brain was calmly telling me that these young lads had gotten the script entirely wrong. You threaten someone with violence if they don't give you what you want…

You don't punch them and then ask. By that point, the leverage is gone. You've already played your ace.

My laughter must have spooked them as they turned and ran.

A passing supermarket delivery van caught most of the interaction on their dashcam. The driver, sensing something was off, stopped. He then waited with me until the police arrived.

The officers took my statement. They took photos of my injuries. And that was that.

No one was ever arrested. The crime remained unsolved.

But it gave me a different perspective on violence. It changed how I viewed the stories I had read all my life.

And I think some of that anger—the anger of the victim left standing in the cold without answers—is likely to have seeped through into the pages of this book.

Because that is the reality of true crime.

It isn't a chessboard. It isn't a game of cat and mouse played by geniuses. It is messy, stupid, and often frighteningly random. It is a punch in the dark.

When I was a boy reading those books, I thought the scary part was the monster. Now, I know the scary part is what follows.

The victims in this book—from the nameless girl in the River Irk to Elizabeth Short—didn't get the dashcam footage. They didn't get to laugh at the absurdity of it all. They didn't get to walk away. They were swallowed by the grey areas of history, by the apathy of cities that moved on too fast.

In many ways, I wrote this book for them.

I wrote it to drag them out of the footnotes and put them back in the light. Because if we can't give them justice, and if we can't give them closure, the very least we can do is give them our attention.

We can refuse to look away.

And we can acknowledge them as people, who had hopes and dreams, friends and families.

Real living people, not characters in a story, but flesh and blood whose lives were cut tragically, violently, short.

And we can make sure that, when it comes to true crime, the focus is on the victim.

If you've enjoyed this book please check out "Strange Britain" on social media for my latest live storytelling events, which include a ten city "Unsolved" themed tour to accompany this book, which will also be touring off and on throughout 2026, and Sheffield's regular Ghost Tours of which I am the host.

And also check out the other books in the Strange Britain series, including The Sins of Sheffield, a true crime book exploring some of the weirder cases from Victorian Sheffield.

Printed in Dunstable, United Kingdom